TERMINUS STATE

NINE MEALS FROM ANARCHY

By DJ Cooper

Angryeaglepublishing.com
Alstead, NH

Copyrights

Dedication

For my children
Chris & Jamie

Find other authors of the apocalypse here:
https://www.facebook.com/groups/writtenapocalypse

"There are only nine meals between mankind and anarchy."

-Alfred Henry Lewis, c.1906

Contact the Author

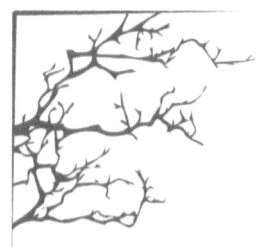

In a moment

My entire body shook. Engulfed by a violent shiver as my awareness of the woods that surrounded me grew. The loud crack of a branch snapping echoed through the trees, confusing my senses. The sound seemed to be coming from everywhere at once. I sat rigid, my Kimber 9mm poised and at the ready. Stiff and motionless, frozen. My eyes, the only movement I dared make. They darted back and forth scanning the area. I had to think, to act; figure out where the sound came from.

All my searching at first revealed nothing and the eerie feeling crept in from all sides. I was not alone. My body rigid so long my muscles began to ache. Eyes the only things allowed to move darted left at the exact moment movement registered. Quick enough to catch a glimpse of the first figure darting between two trees. The glare from the pure white snow blinding me, I had to squint to block the light and questioned if I'd actually seen it. Someone was following us. I was sure I'd seen the movement but lost sight of them in the sunlight. Straining to focus, to identify anything out of place my eyes frantically searched for the figure. Nothing struck me as off, but he was there, I knew it... behind some tree or obscured in the light. Stalking us. Hunting us.

Without realizing it I'd been holding my breath and knew better. Mal's voice in my head reminded me, *"Be calm... listen."* Completely silent, I scanned the sea of brown tree trunks and waited, for something, some movement, a sound, indication of who was out there. It surprised me when to my left another figure ran across a span between two trees. "There you are." My eyes followed them, fixed on both as they moved between the trees. Something told me they were untrained. I was more confident, sure they didn't even know what they were doing. Moving loudly and not in the least bit stealthy, from tree to tree. The way these two moved was haphazard, undisciplined, and sloppy. They were searching, but not looking. Their movements were confusing and a little troubling.

A spot on the snow caught my attention, and my eyes rose following the footprints off into the woods. My footprints. The depressions in the snow marked a trail that was unmistakable a blind man could follow it. The tracks would give us away, and even if they missed those, surely the droplets of blood that blanketed the white floor of the forest would lead them right to us. "How could I be so stupid?"

Were it not for the lucky shot catching us off guard, we would have made short work of this imbecile back at the truck but instead, here I stood staring at the well-marked trail I'd left for them. The struggle had gone awry, and we made for the woods in the wake of an explosion that was close enough to knock Malachi down. When my thoughts returned to what was done to the sweet old woman, the anger inside me boiled into a rage. I prayed through gritted teeth for him to come into my sights. A quick glimpse and he would be mine! Recalling the sight made my body tense. My fears of this encounter had subsided and been replaced with rage!

Now there were two.

A low moan beside me shifted my anger to worry. If I didn't hurry and escape this mess, and somehow get him to the others, he'd soon be gone. The medic, also our local veterinarian, triage the wound. The makeshift hospital room offered some hope and that was my only concern. Worry furrowed my brow, anxiety that I'd lose him gripped my thoughts; I needed to hurry.

He'd always protected and kept me safe. Now it was my turn—I had to help him. Tears stung my eyes and clouded my vision as I strained to peer around the downed tree where we'd taken cover.

I never knew the sound of a bullet passing too close until that moment. At first, I had no idea where the sound came from. The bullet whizzed by, close enough to move the long strands of hair that escaped the bun and dangled whimsically in the light breeze. Before I'd even registered what happened, the sound echoed through the trees. As though an automatic reaction, my body flattened to the ground behind the tree, sprawled across his body. He still lay unconscious on the red sled I'd stolen from outside the Dollar General.

I had to do something. Now! Crouching, I shimmied over and took cover behind a mighty oak tree. I peered around the side farthest from where I'd laid across Malachi. The large pine's extensive base shielded me while I scanned the woods ahead, trying to find the source of the gunfire.

Time seemed to slow to a crawl as I sat and listened. My eyes darted left to right, I sensed nothing; silence. No shots fired and I was confused. I strained to hear. Closing my eyes, tilting my head, and zeroing in on any sounds. A muffled voice weaved amongst the trees. I could almost make out the sounds; a quiet cursing hung on the air. Something had stopped them.

I shimmied once again on my belly across the open area between the trees to another hulking bull pine twenty feet or so to the right. Sliding with as much stealth as the surroundings would allow, until I'd reached a position where the pair was in sight. My teeth gritted at every sound made from the scratching and scrunching of my body weight on top of the snow.

I caught sight of him, my eye twitched, and a low growl rose in my throat. He stood awkwardly, his blubberous belly hanging from beneath his jacket. He held the rifle out in front of himself, bashing at the weapon with the heel of his hand. I almost laughed at the sight; the

arrogance of these people was only exceeded by their stupidity. I began
to wonder if the gun was jammed, or perhaps he couldn't figure out
how to chamber the next round. Then I spotted her, there she stood
cursing at him, the surly waitress with her perpetual sneer.

I remember you, I thought. *I remember both of you.*

I eyed the pistol in my hand. Holding the shiny metal pistol out
and turning it over in my grasp. I was not quite close enough to have
a clean shot with this 9 mm. I had to get closer. Scanning every detail
of the area for cover, the next closest tree with enough to offer any
cover was only a few feet from them. There was no way to shimmy
over and not be seen. My eyes darted left and right seeking the perfect
position to launch an assault, but the area had nothing but small trees,
this section of woods must have been logged in the recent past.

I couldn't wait. If this asshole figured out how to load that gun,
we'd be in deep trouble. Turning back to where he lay on the sled,
wishing for a way out of this, I stood and readied myself to go for the
tree and take the shot. I have to neutralize this here and now if I am
going to make the camp.

My legs were numb from crouching in the snow and didn't want to
move. Dammit, now I wished I'd grabbed my bibs. Leaving them was
stupid on my part; my knees were so cold. I willed them to heed my
command and launch me to that tree.

Once I broke cover, I ran full strides, tripping a few times over
buried sticks and debris on the forest floor. I made it to the tree almost
losing my balance slipping on a patch of snow-covered leaves. The
element of surprise was lost, but they had nowhere to hide. I was a
mere twenty feet away when I took aim at the man, a fumbling idiot
jamming the bolt of the gun forward, never latching the round into
place.

I grabbed hold of a small broken branch stub with my left hand
and leaned around the other side of the tree. Not taking time to aim,
I squeezed off three rounds, hitting him with two in the chest. The

sneer on the face of the waitress changed to shock, and then fear as she looked in my direction. She reached for the rifle as I emerged from behind the tree. The end of the rifle in my direction, the barrel shaking, she pulled the trigger. Looked at the gun in shock and pounded the bolt over and over.

I walked right up to her and snatched the thing from her hands.

This one was his favorite, and I'd have it back. I pulled the bolt back ejecting the spent casing and loading a new round.

I'd turned to leave her where she stood, but in anger, spun back around and with the butt of the gun hit her in the head... hard, knocking her down. I shouldered the weapon, spat at her, and proceeded to go collect my red sled along with the bleeding man.

That was a mistake I'll never make again.

She lunged at me, blood trickling from her eyebrow, making the rage and hatred on her face appear as pure evil. She knocked me to the ground, jerking at the gun and pulling the rifle from my arm. Again, she raised the weapon to me and pulled the trigger. And again, nothing happened. I'd engaged the safety.

Twice, she'd have killed me without remorse.

Without expression, I unholstered my Kimber and in a single motion, raised the gun, disengaged the safety, and pulled the trigger.

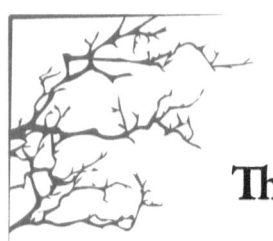

Three Days Earlier

"Would you like some breakfast? I have eggs... Wait, we have no bacon; an omelet?" The crisper drawers opened and closed one at a time.

"Dang, there isn't much to put in an omelet either." Looking up at him, I shrugged and gave a sheepish smile.

I realized I'd forgotten to stop at the grocery store even after he'd sent the list. There was nothing in the fridge worth eating, I cursed under my breath. It was my turn and I'd not picked up any food for the weekend at all, let alone stuff for a decent breakfast; and on the only morning available to spend some time together.

"What do you say we try that little place up at the circle? I love small diners; they have the best food." Coyly winking at him, I closed the door to the fridge behind me.

As usual, he smiled and said, "Your call, I'd eat a bowl of cereal."

This was something that I found endearing, the way he would be happy to hang out. I must admit we often looked like a mismatched pair. I stood in front of him, all five foot, five... *and a half,* of me. I would always add the extra half-inch to appear taller. I marveled at the way this towering man with tattoos and long dark hair would be so gentle. One might think he was trouble at first sight, but that was what I found intriguing.

I recalled how we spent our first date at the range. All that macho man gear for his guns and ammo and yet he opened all the doors and showed off what a gentleman he was. It was the things that many find insignificant like this that affected the way I might look at a suitor.

From one of sighing through a night waiting for it to end, to a manner that might be one of intrigue and interest.

He looked at me and raised an eyebrow, I smirked and hurried to get my gear. We quickly got dressed in our winter gear and headed out the door, twenty minutes later; for the weather had gone from cold to arctic overnight. Me in wedge-heeled boots and a long black wool coat with a scarf wrapped about my neck. He in a hooded Carhartt sweatshirt, his Kimber affixed to his side, and work boots.

The sight of us together may have made one question our compatibility. Lady and the Tramp never seemed so poignant and yet fascinating as people often noted his devotion and gentle nature.

The cold had settled into the area and at a brisk ten degrees the parking lot now resembled an ice arena, and me without any skates. Clinging to his arm for stability, I considered that my decision to wear heeled boots may have been a less than stellar choice. I'd made it to the relative safety of the truck without crashing to the ground in spectacular fashion. Grasping my arm, he hoisted me into the tall cab, and we were off to the quaint diner for a bite.

Over the past week we'd been so busy that it seemed as though we made little effort for even simple things like phone calls. Driving a limo had its downfalls. Working until the wee hours of the morning, but then waking up at seven for a short airport run left me tired. Him, with his usual night shift, meant he was long gone to sleep before I'd even made the airport. Some mornings even a phone call was not something we could swing.

Days would go by where our only communication was a few texts from either end. One might indeed wonder how we managed to maintain a relationship. Looking at the schedule it was easy to put into perspective. He worked nights, and me? Well best put, I worked on a whim! It made the time we spent together a premium and I hated it when things would go wrong. We worked with this kind of scheduling problem and weekends were the times when every moment mattered.

We hardly got to spend time with each other much, if at all, during the week; so our weekends were like gold. In the limo world these were busy days and today I would savor every moment. I had the entire weekend off and was not about to waste what time we had.

When we got to the diner the lot was full, which I took to be a good sign. This usually meant the food would be delicious. Sliding into a tight space with his gigantic red truck he moved fast to get past the people standing around when he came to the passenger's side and opened the door for me, offering his hand to help me down from the cab. He even opened the door for me to enter the diner, and as he did a warm breeze flowed from the opening that carried a scent of bacon with a hint of something in the oven. Oh, how wonderful the scents that hovered in the air smelled as we entered, and they caught me by surprise. My stomach began to rumble.

It was full, and after a couple laps around the dining area we found a small table in the free-for-all seating set towards the back of the small restaurant; a single table with two chairs. The parking lot had not lied, the tables were full of people. We passed by the counter, a couple sat with coffees and their tablets. In the corner an older gentleman had his paper held up reading, I presumed he was waiting for his food. For a place full of people there was not much chatting going on. Many had their phones out, or a laptop, busily working. One couple had a table full of tech, but incredibly enough, they were verbally communicating with one another.

I sniffed the air as we considered our favorites from the menu. The pancakes seemed like the ticket on such a chilly day. Blueberry pancakes and I'd have them garnished with real maple syrup. Perfect. This combination of flavors would be mouthwatering.

My anticipation was evident, waiting for the waitress so that I could order the savory tastes of the tart blueberries and sticky, sweet real maple flavor. In my whimsy I could imagine the greasy kitchen; the hot stove littered with eggs, pancakes, and bacon... splattering its greasy rain as it danced atop the grill.

The waitress approached, placing her hand on the back of my guy's chair. He leaned away, flashing her a disgusted look, that she ignored as she leaned over him.

She seemed pleasant, asking, "Can I start you guys with some coffee?"

"Yes please," I piped up. "And can I also have a glass of water?"

Still considering the menu, he nodded to her. I smiled a genuine smile at her, "Make it two? Please."

She grunted, turned, and retreated to the waitress station.

We sat chatting while we awaited our coffee. Mal checked out the surroundings, like he always did. It was as if he was casing the place making sure he knew where the nearest exits were. "This seems like a pretty good place, have you been here before?"

"No, I'd seen this place but never stopped. I must admit I've been curious, I thought about giving it a try but glad I waited."

"Do you know what you want?"

"Yep, it'll be pancakes for me."

"I thought you were thinking about omelets at the house. You sure you don't want one?"

"I can't." I said smirking my lips, "I'm allergic to the regular eggs. I can only eat the organic ones. You know, the ones that come from chickens that are allowed to run around? They don't have all the hormones and antibiotics in them."

"Ahhh yes, I do recall. Little miss organic over here." He laughed.

"Hey now! Don't poke fun." I retorted.

He grinned and grasped my hand across the table giving me a wink as our waitress returned with the coffees and water. "You ready to order?"

I looked up, and she stood over us, a lax posture, and bored expression. Pad in hand, pen at the ready she awaited our order. The tasty odors had me craving bacon with my pancakes. I was ready, sure of what I wanted to order. "Yes,"

We'd each ordered our meal and sat enjoying the wonderful coffee. On the walls were hand-painted murals of farm life. He pointed out a section with a barn and some chickens and made fun of my egg fetish. Well, it was really an all-food fetish, but he only liked to tease me about things like eggs, and butter. The only vegetables we had were always fresh, not canned and once I'd made him put back a steak in favor of a grass fed one that was significantly more expensive. Sometimes he didn't understand, I mused, and shot him a look, pretending to be angry at his comments about the eggs. I wasn't mad but scowled at him for laughing at my indignant look.

She'd returned and brought his plate, and I was impressed. Across the table his breakfast consisted of a sizeable steak with a couple of eggs, some home fries, and pristine toast laid across the massive platter, neatly segregated, yet brushing each other as though it were doing a ballet across the plate for his enjoyment.

The imminent arrival of the next plate was at hand, and for sure, the plate of pancakes would be steaming hot slabs of fluffy, lightly browned, flavored with vanilla perfect pancakes. My mouth watered as I waited on edge for them. Donning those sweet-smelling disks would be telltale dark blue spots of the largest and ripest blueberries. The napkin was laid out neatly upon my lap, for this was the ladylike thing to do. I was ready. I awaited the feast.

Like an opera I spied her in the distance, the pudgy blonde waitress strode, gliding across the floor; my meal in hand, coming straight for the table. A broad smile emerged as she laid the plate on the table. I looked down and my smile diminished when I saw the single pat of butter sitting atop the two flat slabs with black specks haphazardly dotting their tops.

My disappointment was evident with the change in my expression. The flaccid pancake drooped lazily off one side of the plate as the small pat of butter disappeared into a hole dead center. Such a marked difference in the two meals. This seemed tragic that my expectations were dashed in such a way.

No matter, it was a lovely day with breakfast and conversation to enjoy. Trying to disguise my disappointment, I looked to her. " Can I please get some extra butter?"

She glared in my direction, huffed, turned on her heel, and without a word she retreated from whence she came. A bit later she returned, the scowl on her face had not changed. A single piece of her stringy blonde hair hung across her furrowed brow as she pulled two small containers of Country Crock Margarine from her stained white apron. She dropped them on the table in my direction, before turning to my boyfriend.

Her demeanor changed markedly, and she smiled, asking him. "How's your coffee, sweetie?"

He grunted at her without looking up and pointed to the two small cups on the table, "Babe, you know that's margarine. You don't eat that."

I was impressed that for all his funning, he paid attention and considered my food choices. But the waitress stared hard at me as though I'd cast her in a bad light. I wondered what I'd done to make her so disagreeable towards me.

I struggled to disguise the look of disgust and my voice stuttered. "This... is fine every once in a while."

We'd discussed the differences while shopping only last week. He liked Country Crock, but I'd refused to buy it, having called it "practically plastic." It was enough for me that he'd remembered.

Looking down at my very flat pancake and then to my wonderful man, I smiled. He'd not cared what she'd done, only that my food was what I'd wanted. We didn't get much time like this, with him working nights during the week and me having to work weekends often; so, when we visited, we tried to make the most of the time we had together. I was not going to allow any of these issues to spoil the day.

Food service was often a tiresome job. Customers always complaining, stiffing hard working servers on the tip. Servers would run from table to table checking on details, gathering up used plates, refilling drinks, and fetching desserts. Often standing for eight or more hours in a shift and walking miles during the course of their travels around the eatery.

So why be surly to a customer? Perhaps she'd had a grueling day or perhaps she'd perceived our table as being lousy tippers even though no indication alluded to that as a reason. All I did know was that there was no reason for her to be so annoyed.

I poured the roughly two tablespoons of real maple syrup on the pancakes and tried to stretch it out. After eating about a quarter of one pancake, the maple syrup had disappeared, sucked up by the pancakes like a sponge. I sat considering the possibility of requesting more from this surly woman who'd chosen to stand but twenty feet away and chat with another while watching my obvious displeasure yet pretending not to notice. Or... I could live with the brown colored corn syrup that was offered at the table.

I'd only wanted a pleasurable morning, and this was turning out to be a genuine detriment to my psyche. Rather than face off against the gruff waitress, I opted for the lesser of miseries by choosing the table syrup rather than invoke the wrath of the waitress again. Grasping the translucent plastic ketchup style bottle with the brown sticky syrup inside, I tipped it upside down and prepared to squeeze out a string of this thick ooze onto my flat slabs flecked with black spots.

Waiting for the goo to slide to the tip of the bottle, my thoughts trailed off. "*This was not how I'd intended to have breakfast.*" As I awaited the slow descent toward the opening of the container, again I thought about how I'd not gone shopping, and found myself full of remorse for my short sightedness. After this fiasco, I would not be remiss in this task again, or I'd likely better be prepared to face another bout of waitress rage.

Our waitress was laughing with another at the waitress station while rolling up some silverware into napkins. No indication of anxiety or angst between them that could be outwardly seen.

The syrup had made its way to the cap and was ready to be applied to the pancake slabs. Grasping the bottle, I gave a squeeze.

Plop!

The top had not been screwed on the bottle properly and I now had a deluge of gelatinous brown, sticky liquid oozing over the sides of the plate, onto the table, and headed for my lap in a slow creeping motion. Looking about the room of tables, searching for a savior with those ever present white soggy towels and for once none were to be seen anywhere. No one. The waitress had gone missing as I sat looking at the floating rafts in my plate and contemplating how to avoid the wave which was headed for me in a slow-motion slide toward the table edge.

He looked first to my plate and then to my face. The combination of gelatinous slime headed for me at a crawl, horror filled my eyes as I tried to build a dam to divert the river anywhere but toward my lap. This struggle with the syrup must have been quite a sight. He laughed and offered me his napkin.

"What happened?"

"I don't know, the top came off." I said with some panic in my voice.

"Why are you eating that crap anyway?"

"Cause the waitress is so bitchy, I didn't want to deal with asking for more syrup."

He shook his head and looked around the room. The old lady from the next table brushed back a wandering piece of her white hair with her tiny, crooked fingers and offered me her napkin with a smile. I thanked her and weakly returned her smile.

The realities of the consequences of my failure to obtain the proper food items became more and more urgent in my thoughts. If I'd only gotten the stuff to cook us breakfast, I wouldn't be here right now. The waitress sauntered over and asked my man if his food was ok, ignoring my precarious position with the ooze closing in on me. I was becoming angry, thinking to myself *"Is his food ok? Are you freaking kidding me?"*

I cut her off. "Can I have a rag for this?" Feeling as though I'd done something wrong, I began to explain. "The top... It popped right off."

She rolled her eyes as she wadded up the place mat and told me to lift my plate of floating pancake rafts, so she could wipe.

I'd become a little less than patient at this point and handed the whole mess to her saying, "I'm finished, thank you."

She wiped up some of the deluge but left the rolled-up place mat and a huge swath of the now-stable, sticky brown goo on the table in front of me. Then she placed the check on the side and left, never to return.

We sat, looking at the mess of a table, questioning how we'd gotten to this point. I'd waited many a table over the years and to witness bad service never got any easier.

I tried to figure out what caused her surly nature but was at a loss.

A small unassuming voice called from the next table, "Perhaps, she liked your guy friend and treating you like crap is how she thought she would win his attention."

"Wha...?" I looked over at the old lady.

"I saw you looking with that confused look. Perhaps, she doesn't have a clue what she's doing, and you interrupted her smoke break, she reeked of smoke." The smiling white-haired old lady grinned as she spoke.

Malachi wasn't happy with the service. "She's getting no tip," he said, annoyed.

When rising to leave I said, "As a matter of fact? I've got the tip."

He turned to me and raised his eyebrows in confusion. "Really?"

I pulled a bill out of my wallet and slapped the thing down on the table—hard. Right in the sticky mess she'd left behind, making sure the entire bill was slathered in the lovely slime of brown goo. Wiping my hands, I smiled at him and took his arm to go.

The old woman, pointed to the bill, smiled, and said, "That's how it's done, honey."

Smiling to myself as we walked past the waitress and out the door, she had the nerve to wink at us. My guy grasped my arm before opening the door for me. Pausing for a second and looking toward the waitress, I smooched him on his scruffy cheek and said, "Thank you, darlin."

My precious time with my boyfriend had been spent battling a surly waitress while staving off the wave of brown goo. If only I'd been more conscientious, I could have made even better food myself. The many times during the meal where I'd wished I'd not forgotten to stop made me realize how much more pleasant it is to have a peaceful meal at home.

The ways our busy lives intruded on personal moments grew until none remained. We were working separate shifts, we didn't need to be battling servers, or some other thing that would rob us of the little time we had penciled in for one another. The world had become disconnected, even with all its connections people didn't know how to act in real personal situations.

My thoughts drifted to the waitress, who acted out in spectacular fashion, the others eating, each in their own little area of their table, never reaching out to the others nearby. The mother and daughter who sat staring at their phones as they mindlessly shoveled scrambled eggs into their gaping mouths. The one old man seated at the counter, eating alone.

Didn't anyone take notice of the murals on the wall, the farm, the community where people visited with each other at the fence? I wondered if any of it was real, if anyone spied the couple that struggled with a deluge of muck advancing in slow motion.

Once, back when people spoke to one another, a time when people would regard their surroundings, the struggling couple would have been a cause for concern; but no more. The waitress would hurry over and correct the issue, bringing a fresh plate. Others around would laugh at the spectacle and take bets on if the brown sticky river would reach the lap of the frazzled woman. No one cared anymore, except perhaps the little old lady. She'd lived those days. She remembered. Sunday dinners and church suppers. The memories reflected in her eyes, the connection in the one comment. She understood.

A thoughtful smile emerged on my face as I thought of the little old lady. Only a few words passed between us, but she'd taken in all the goings on. This tiny woman with pure white hair, had spoken. *"That's how it's done, honey."* I smiled.

Maybe, just maybe... breakfast was not all that bad after all.

That day, like most other days, we would scroll through social media posts about politics and foreign affairs, who did what that offended whom, and why we couldn't post any good memes anymore. FanPages social media site had come down hard on anything deemed to be outside of their acceptability standards; standards that seemed to be subjective and inconsistent. We could play a video of an animal being abused, but God forbid if anyone poked fun at a screaming politician. The media now censored everything, the content either too graphic for the public's overly sensitive eyes or considered too controversial and might mislead the public opinion.

It was all now little more than a circus, the three rings spinning incessantly riling up this group or that demographic. As if on some center stage upon which the action was played out for all. No ring master in charge of the spectacle, only the clowns directing the action; orchestrating every move, directing every event or issue to incite the people. Oh, the spectacle of the political circus and we the people would stand and cheer. As each act was unveiled in the political merry-go-round, the pandering would begin. Let all who would hear, come close, and witness the next false event to distract the masses.

In some odd fashion things became extreme and almost crazy. Someone somewhere was offended by something and people needed legislating for every facet of their lives. I'd been waiting for the true craziness to begin, for the pure silliness to take that center ring. We could all stand and witness the show as the circus began its next spectacle.

Welcome to the stage, the newest disgruntled group of people who need accommodation from the average guy. The guy with the house that has a yard of sand takes the stage; he claims that the house with grass is ruining his life because the grass wants to grow amidst his spectacularly worry free smooth golden waves. The slender green shoots rising from beneath the small yellow grit to create the unsightly speckled mottling of colors. This is an infringement on my space he screams.

"Yell it brother!" shouts the guy across the street.

He was triggered and the neighborhood must stick together.

"Oh, the tragedy of grass, the green evil encroaches and infringes on my space. Ban all grass for this is the root of all ecological tragedy. Here! I have a paper written by a non-ecologist to prove my point."

Now the town meets, but all grassland owners are excluded because the assumption is that they cannot be impartial. The decision is swift and decisive, the grass grower is a bigot who hates all people with sand yards and is plotting to have grass take over the neighborhood. All of the neighbors are shocked and begin to shun him. It is declared: All yards must look like other yards and be free from grass! The signs pop up amongst the other political pandering telling us to vote for the grass ban.

This worked for straws; plastic straws have now been replaced with paper ones, standing proud, rising up in defiance of plastic and waving high above the rim standing out as a beacon of hope in an ecologically compromised world... straight out of their—*plastic cups.*

We've dictated the yards people walk on, like we decided what they will drink with, what fast foods should be outlawed because they are fattening, and which history to allow and what history to eradicate.

The monumental implications of those wide-sweeping and oppressive legislations that had been gaining momentum are terrifying. With the new tendency to over-legislate the populous for fear of offending someone—anyone; anything and everything we do was now legislated and regulated. So much so, that people had become afraid to take a step without permission. Some days I wondered if George Orwell had been some kind of a prophet.

Again, the view was the same with this latest goal; this one was to ban weapons, all of them. The plan wasn't good enough to only go after the second amendment anymore; they'd decided arrows, knives, and even decorative antique swords were implements of mass destruction. "*Ban it all, end the violence.*" the signs said.

The new legislation being laid out to take away the people's right to bear arms had created a canyon between the candidates and their supporters. Not a divide or even a rift—but a vast, open void between two extremes. The election was coming tomorrow, and a new President would be elected. Every four years brand new candidates emerged, but this year eight of them took the podiums. Political parties sprang up from all walks of life, each screaming their own agenda. All vying for the most coveted seat in town.

Elected—Pfft... What a joke. There were no real elections anymore. We had more voters that paid no taxes, were sitting in prison, were dead, or were in the country illegally, than we had taxpayers at this point. All offered a handsome price by some man behind a curtain pulling the puppet's strings; bought and paid to pick a candidate. Those who paid no tax, instead collecting each month from the stupendous general fund were the ones deciding where tax dollars went; now that became the true circus.

I feared for our land because it seemed that no matter who was elected, what would follow could only be a civil war. The media was playing on this for all it was worth, and neighbors were beginning to choose sides. Entire communities had begun cordoning off the roads in and out of their neighborhoods. Some homeowners had been run from their homes in areas where they did not fit into the political leaning of their neighbors. *What have we become?* I wondered.

We picked up a few extras in our wanderings, most definitely food; I would have no more pancake fiascos. We would likely stay close to home for now, but I still felt as though we wouldn't be prepared for what was coming.

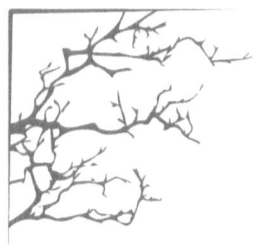

Election Day

I took the weekend off and planned on staying home. But after yesterday's pancake calamity, and the chaos that we'd seen as we drove about the area leaf peeping, I decided to take the whole week off. This was mostly because Mal didn't want me driving in and out of Boston around the time of the election, but I was glad to be home for more than just a weekend.

We rose early in the morning to do our civic duty... to vote, in spite of the fact that I wasn't even sure it counted anymore. The air was crisp with the scent of snow and most of the leaves were soon to be gone from the trees. Many could be seen tumbling in flashes of yellow and red; across yards and roadways, heralding the coming of winter.

We breezed through the local donut drive-through for a coffee and bagel, we would have no omelets today either. We wanted to get this over with as fast as possible, we'd started out early in hopes of beating any crowds that might gather. We drove into town and headed straight to our local voting station, but even in a small New England town such as ours we could see that there was already minor mayhem in the making.

Screaming people with signs lined each side of the walkway leading to the entrance of the building and beyond, stretching as close as they could to the voting booths. "Aren't they supposed to be no closer than 150 feet from the polling place?" I asked as I gripped Mal's arm tighter. On the one side a loud woman was screaming almost in my face. Her expression was twisted in anger as spittle flew from her lips. She was consumed with the hatred of others who didn't agree with her.

Waving her brightly polished fake fingernail at me she screamed, "If you don't vote for what is right, you are the one at fault when the next disaster happens!"

I hissed back at her. "If people acted right and didn't try to bully others... or try to force them into their way of thinking, it is conceivable that there wouldn't be any!"

I would not be bullied or harassed into voting in a particular way, and the behavior? Frankly, it just plain ticked me off that someone would be screaming at me like that. She stood glaring at me as the line slowly progressed. From the other side of the walkway a man in an odd uniform I'd never seen before, shouted obscenities to a group of practically prepubescent voters who'd been taunting him. I observed them and wondered if they were even old enough to vote. All walks of life stood in line together for a single purpose, yet the division was stark.

There would be no middle ground today. No civility, not even the fake niceties that most people offered in civilized societies were performed. It was then that I knew for sure... this day would not end well. I was certain that the very fabric of society had been broken today, and my hopes of a civilized election were dashed.

We still had anxiety from the diner, only yesterday it was still quite fresh in our minds. Oh... the diner. I was a little annoyed by that experience, even a day later, and preoccupied with the thought of the waitress flirting with my boyfriend. I chuckled a little, because later he told me that he knew all along what she was doing and acted oblivious on purpose. The experience served to accentuate the stark shift in our society. The changes in the ways that people viewed community and how we interacted. Thoughts of that pancake fiasco brought moments of humor alternating with irritation, but overall, even that was a better day than this promised to be.

I stood in line going over the day's errands in my head, lamenting on the pancakes, and otherwise oblivious to those around me. A sharp noise behind me brought me back into the moment. There was some shouting going on. A momentary anxiety gripped me until I glanced back to see what was happening. Horror shook me inside when I beheld that sweet little old white-haired lady from the diner. She stood out of line looking down with her black patent leather purse clutched close to her chest.

A young couple were pointing at her and shouting. "Get out of here old woman, your generation screwed this country up. Now is our time." They threw leaves and sticks at her and as I stood and watched, the real terror came over me. The younger woman reached out and smacked the old lady, shoving her harshly, making her stumble and fall into the fence.

I turned to look at Mal, but he was gone. At six foot three he was an imposing figure. By the time I'd located him he stood toe to toe with one of them holding him by the scruff of his neck. He towered over the young troublemakers and threatened to give back to them what they'd offered the lady. They cowered in his presence but once he'd helped the lady up and ushered her forward in the line to stand with us, they began to shout insults again.

"Typical," I said. "They're all balls and badass from a distance."

The people behind us objected to her cutting in line, but a glare from both of us ended any other comment. We escorted the woman to the voting booth and stood guard for her to vote and then took our turns. We then walked her to her car, and as was his usual, he opened her door and helped her in. "Will you be alright?"

She smiled warmly and offered a quick tilt of her head. "Yes, I'm sure I'll be fine." She then looked to each of us with her wise eyes. A person could see the years in the pale green stare, the crepe of her skin as it lay on her face showed a long time full of laugh lines. She'd seen some stuff in her lifetime, that was evident in her expression.

"Please," I said. "Let me give you my phone number. If you have any troubles, phone me right away."

"Thank you both for all of your help." She gave a tilt of her head and her eyes lit up as the memory inserted itself into her thoughts. "I remember you." She smiled. "You're the pancakes."

We all laughed, and she filled us in on what happened after we left. "That curt waitress? She didn't come to clean the table right away. We were also left to sit; she never even cleared the plates or warmed our coffee." The woman tilted her head and a sadness washed across her face. "We were long done but had to wait to get the bill so we could pay, so we sat watching the people come and go." A twinkle glistened in her eye and she gave us a bit of a sly grin.

I caught the look and anxiously waited for her to recount what happened. She giggled a small giggle and winked at me.

"When that waitress did come back to bring our bill, she looked surprised that there was a tip on your table and snatched the bill up, shoving it directly into her pocket." She put her small, crooked fingers up to her face to shroud another giggle. "It took her a moment to realize the thing was dripping with syrup." A sly smirk emerged, and she winked knowingly at me. "If only you could have seen her face. It was worth the wait to catch the look." Her small hand went to her mouth once again and she laughed heartily.

We both had a good laugh with her and I said, "Karma."

She reached out for my hand. Her frail crooked fingers were cold to touch, the skin so soft it felt as a feather's light brush, but also weathered from years of work.

I was overcome with worry for her. "Please make sure you call if you need anything." I urged.

She smiled and promised she would.

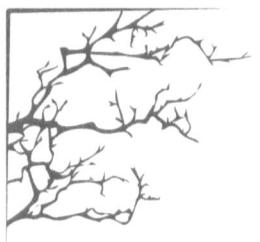

Stuff To Do

We watched her as she drove away, then had to push our way through the volatile crowd as we headed for the truck on the other side of the building. Holding his arm, I gave it a squeeze; I was more thankful for him than he could even know at that moment. He opened the door as usual for me, and before I climbed in I paused and looked back towards the line where someone yelled out how oppressed I was for having my door opened. Scrunching my eyes to see where the insult came from, I felt sad. Sad for all the people who fell for the drivel. Sad that even chivalry was now a dreadful thing. Sad and disgusted.

The shouting and insults had been growing worse, people were screaming into the faces of those nearby, so many belligerent and angry. My eyes full of worry, I looked to him, "This will not go well," I said as I turned and climbed into the passenger seat.

I was never so glad to leave a place as I was that day. We left behind the insults and mayhem to go on about our errands. Our day would be busy with some local friends at the range. We both liked to shoot; but I would often tease him about it. "Oh, you're such a guy," I'd say.

Secretly, I liked to go, but also liked to pretend it was a guy thing, having him go off with the guys to practice or test rounds. Of course, he would pretend he needed to show me how to shoot and I would play along. That was, until he decided one day to get all full of himself and try and show off, making the guys think I couldn't shoot, because... after all, I was only a girl.

I put the headset on and grabbed his Daniel's Defense AR-15, popped in a full mag and commenced to pick off every golf ball on the range. After which, I nonchalantly strolled past, handing him the gun and the headset with a nod on my way by. The moment was perfect, I flicked my long brown hair behind me, looking back to offer him a quick wink, and I sashayed to the picnic table where I'd been sitting chatting with the other women. High fives all around followed by giggles, the ladies were impressed. We sat in solidarity of well shot women everywhere. All of this amused him and we laughed as we waved to our friends and pulled out of the driveway.

Once we left, Mal blurted out, "You know... you didn't have to hit every one of them."

I glared at him, "You didn't have to act as though I couldn't shoot straight."

"Yeah, I know. I sure took a bit of shit from the guys though." He mindlessly checked out the scenery from the windows as we passed.

I suddenly felt bad and reached out for his arm. "Next time, I'll miss a few and we'll call it luck."

"Nahhh, I'm proud of how well you shoot. I shouldn't have tried to show off like that and act like some tough guy."

"You're MY tough guy." I offered.

He smiled at me and we both turned our eyes to the road.

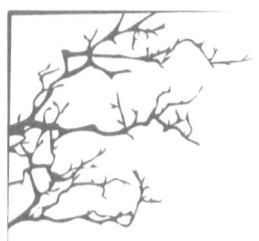

The Store

We'd avoided the news of the day on purpose, but it was hard to avoid it all. The craziness was all over social media with posts and videos. It came in the form of texts from friends, asking had we heard this or that. The election was all that people could talk about everywhere we went.

We stopped for lunch at a small local diner that we often visited and knew the owner well. Chris and Mal have known each other since they were kids. He looked up from the menu at me with an evil twinkle in his eye and raising his eyebrow. "Will you be having pancakes?"

I glared at him for the second time today, "I will NOT be having pancakes... Ever!"

We both laughed and ordered our usual. He had a specialty burger; it was one of his favorites. They made them so fat that even his massive hands struggled to hang on to the thing. He munched and grunted as the juices ran onto his hand. I must admit it looked good; the slight charring on the patty and savory burnt smell was intoxicating.

For myself, I loved their grilled cheese; they added three different kinds of cheese; sandwiched between two slices of soft but crispy Texas toast bread. The salty butter that was seared to the outside to precisely the perfect shade of light brown with a gooey center of cheese oozing from between the layers was heavenly. Added to it all was a steaming plate of seasoned fries that were to die for! The kind of fries that were soft inside with a nice greasy crunchy outer shell. I liked to dip mine in ranch dressing while he preferred plain ole ketchup, calling me weird.

We preferred to eat before doing any food shopping and next week I'd need to return to work. I admit I was thoroughly enjoying my mini stay-at-home vacation and wished for a job that was closer so I could spend less time driving and more at home. Today, we would be shopping not only for weekly groceries but a bit extra and we didn't need to do it hungry. Food prices had skyrocketed over the past few months and we'd been careful not to indulge in junk food, but the food bill was still often higher than we liked.

While we sat finishing up our coffee and discussing our shopping needs, Mal's friend Steve walked into the small diner. He came right up to our table. The look on his face was difficult to discern. It was something between shock and anger, this was offset by his shoulders that were slumped forward as though he were tired.

He looked to each of us and spoke in hushed tones, "Have you been to Keene yet?"

We looked at one another confused. Mal shook his head. "Not yet. We were just getting ready to go."

I nodded in agreement listening in.

"Well, if you're going to go; it'd be best if you get to it. People are getting hot under the collar and tempers are flaring. There have been a few fights and the little boot store downtown had its window smashed in." He leaned forward both hands palm down on the table. He paused, took a deep breath and looked in both directions before he continued. "Make sure you're both," pausing to look at me before continuing, "carrying, and make it fast."

"That fast?" A nervous sweat rushed across my forehead.

His head moved side to side in dismay, "With the way the election is going Dani, I would bet we only have a couple hours till all hell breaks loose. If I were you, I'd get in and get out as quick as possible."

"Do you think it will be that bad?"

He appeared weary and haggard, the look in his eye was hollow; disbelief hung on him like an oversized shirt. "I hope not. But there are some that are begging for all-out war. Screaming and yelling, shoving people. I don't know what they're thinking."

He waved back to us as he left the store, offering a nod to Chris, the store owner.

We paid for our meal and shook Chris's hand. He held on to both our hands and looked right at each of us in turn. "We all could see this was coming," he said nodding with eyebrows raised. "Get a move on now. We are closing but there's a meeting in the back barn tonight to discuss the contingencies."

"See you then," Mal said.

I looked up confused, I had no idea what the man was talking about, yet Mal seemed to be apprised of the meaning. "A meeting?" I glanced at him questions racing through my mind once we got outside.

"Yea... some of the guys that go shooting with us. We've been talking about the issues that have been concerning us surrounding the whole political arena lately."

"Are we going?"

He looked down at me and smiled. "Yes, I suppose we should."

We were walking back to the truck when the man from the store called out. "Malachi." We stopped and looked back towards him. "Let any of the others you talk to know."

"Will do!" he called back.

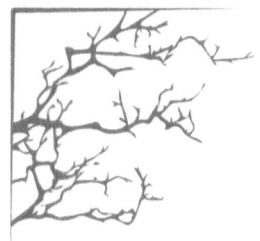

The Town

It was five and a half miles to Keene, and nothing along the trip looked any different than it had the day before. We saw a few people in their yards, some kids playing on a trampoline, and a horse and buggy trotting down the roadway back toward the town from where we'd come.

Until...

We pulled into the parking lot, around the side of the building of the grocery store. And right in the front lot two men were fighting. A full-on fist fight, each swinging and blocking punches. Four or five others stood by, watching the boxing match happening right in the middle of the parking lot. This looked crazy to me, it wasn't something one might find on an afternoon shopping trip. Something had gone wrong in the fabric of society. No matter what they were fighting over, although we were fairly sure we were aware of what it was, this was not how sane, civilized people settled disagreements.

By the time we'd parked and emerged from the vehicle, more had gathered to observe the fight. Some cheered, screaming, red-faced, waving fists in the air; while others stood wringing their hands, trying to quiet the growing mob. This was trouble in the making and we wanted no part of it. We slipped past the crowd and grabbed a shopping cart, whizzing through the automatic doors. When we got to the inner door, I grabbed a separate cart. Mal looked at me confused.

"If we split up and grab what we are looking for things will go faster, and we can get the hell outta here."

"Good idea Dani, you head for the dairy and vegetables and I'll take the other stuff."

"You're on," I said. Standing at the ready, small fingers wrapped around the handle of the cart, edging it forward, like a racer might do awaiting the green light. "Meet you at the checkout," I said with a sly grin before I bolted to the other end of the store.

Shopping cart races were a challenging task that day; every aisle was packed with panicked people grabbing things off the shelves. I stood frozen at the head of one aisle. The one with the coffee and tea, along with breakfast items. A frenzied group had destroyed the aisle in their panic to gather the basics like coffee and cereal. A bag of coffee lay open on the floor with black grounds strewn in a wide sweeping motion from the empty trampled package.

I was stunned, the election was not even over yet, polls were not even showing up and yet the volatile masses had begun to riot. That was what this small altercation in the aisle of a supermarket made me think of. Riots...

These were our neighbors, people we saw every week strolling the aisles for the next week's menu items. Now, they'd turned into lunatics and thugs. One tall man stood over an older lady, screaming with a bag of sugary cereal over his head. His giant gut hung in front of him obscuring his belt line. He used the giant, blubberous mass like a battering ram, shoving people out of the way.

I stood in shock at what I saw, wishing I'd not chosen cart racing today. I glanced in all directions... and masses of people fought and argued all around me. I wanted to make it to the checkout and give up, but the crowd had closed in on me. A ripple of panic rushed over me. This was dangerous and I realized it, perhaps too late. Getting out was the only thing I could focus on. I shifted the cart away from the aisle and bumped another cart.

A young woman turned to me; her face twisted in hate as she screamed at me. "Watch where you're going, bitch!"

I didn't want to be in the middle of any of this. "Excuse me."

She grabbed the end of my cart with both hands and shoved it into my stomach, hard. "Well, then pay attention to where you're going."

A searing pain on the left side of my head slammed me, and I began to feel confused. A circle of darkness crept over me as my knees went weak, I clung to the cart trying to hold myself up. I didn't understand what was happening... everything went dark.

☼ ☼ ☼

Small streams of light fluttered into view as I blinked. "Where am I?"

"You're OK, this is the manager's office." A familiar voice soothed.

Flashes of those moments before waking up danced in my mind, although I struggled to make sense of them. "What happened?

"Take it easy Dani. You were hit in the head with a can."

Another voice, "A can of peas, as near as we can figure."

My vision cleared and I looked to those around me. I was comforted and wrapped my arms around his waist as he sat on the edge of the overstuffed sofa. Mal was right by my side. The swift upright movement made the darkness close in once again and I whimpered into his arms. The pain in my head began to throb. I reached up to the spot where it ached and found a gigantic wad attached to my head.

"Damn head wounds bleed like hell." he said.

"Bleeding?" I questioned.

"Yea, the edge of the can left a fair-sized gash on your head when it hit you. We've got the bleeding stopped for now but you're gonna need stitches."

"Ughhhhh." I groaned and leaned back on the arm of the comfy sofa.

"Do you think you can walk?"

My head swam with pain when I bobbed it up and down. "I think so."

"Well, let's hurry up and take you over to the clinic."

He helped me stand and the store manager grabbed my other arm, together they walked me to the door. I peered out with some trepidation, but inside the store it was calm again. I turned back blinking at the manager. "The store's quiet now."

"Yes, the police showed up to handle the fight outside and came into the store. It was chaos; no one listened to them, even though they were using a bullhorn. One of the younger officers drew his gun and fired right into the ceiling," he said, pointing to the ceiling of the store where two holes opened through the tiles. The man looked almost panicked. "The emergency personnel must be stretched thin. The other officer came in and looked at your head. He said that he thought you'd be ok. There are no ambulances available at the moment, we agreed to see to it that you'd be taken to the hospital or the clinic as soon as possible."

I nodded at the man with a blank face and continued to gaze about the disheveled store. Many of the aisles had products on the floor, some were opened, with contents spilled out. Workers with their red vests moved from aisle to aisle, retrieving the downed items and placing them back on the shelves. Some went around sweeping or mopping up the messes.

We approached the exit doors, but they did not open automatically into the breezeway as usual. The manager had to open it with keys. A glance behind me spotted two people with sober faces checking out at the register. I looked at the man ready to ask about what happened, but he answered.

"We've decided on ten people shopping at any time in the store for now. When one leaves another can be admitted."

I nodded and took a seat on the bench that sat near the outer windows. The others went to the man at the main door and chatted before each left in different directions.

The manager paused at the bench I was seated on, "He will be back with the vehicle in a few moments, are you ok here by yourself? I need to run inside the store, but I'll be right back."

I nodded.

The scene outside was surreal, a line of people peering in at me through the glass doors. Some wore faces of fear, while others radiated anger and malice. A loud bang surprised me, and my head jerked toward the set of doors on the other end. A man and a woman were trying to break the glass on the doors, while a crowd of ten or more onlookers stood and cheered.

Was this it? Was this how riots and looting began? My mind raced and I shivered. It was getting cold and I so wished they would come back. The man at the main entrance swung around with a shotgun in his hands. He raised it and aimed as he walked towards the pair. Noting his presence, they both put their hands up and stepped back, feigning shock and indignation, as though they were somehow innocent and detached from the situation.

The woman looked familiar, but my mind was fuzzy. I knew I'd seen her before but I couldn't think straight. I reached up to touch the gash on my head as the store manager returned.

"Don't touch it or it may begin to bleed again" he said in a tone that made me feel like he was chiding me.

Another bang, but this time on the first set of doors. Mal was back. My heart leapt with joy, it meant we could leave this place and these people. I felt bad for the store manager, but I wanted to get out of here.

The man with the shotgun waved his hand at him, motioning for him to pull around to the other set of doors where the crowd was gone. He pulled the truck right up next to the doors and the manager helped him load the groceries we'd bought. I assumed he'd checked out the stuff I had in my cart; it was all in the bags. I wish I'd known what had happened, I was so confused, it was unsettling.

After he was done, he returned for me. I stood a little wobbly but on my own two feet. We began walking toward the door and paused. I looked at the manager, his brow was furrowed, and he looked tired. "Thank you for everything" I said.

"No trouble at all Missy, get on over to the hospital and have that head looked at."

"Will you be alright?" My voice quivered, gazing at the crowds waiting for entrance, I became worried for him.

"I'll be ok. I got more help on the way to make sure the store is secure, don't you worry."

I thanked him again and with a little help we exited the store. I was thinking while making my way to the truck. We got outside and I stood against the wall while Mal opened the door for me.

A woman reached out and pulled my hair, sneering. "What's wrong? The little princess can't even open her own door?"

I remembered her. Her pulling of my hair caused my wound to separate, blood began making a slow path down my forehead and diverted at my eyebrow. It began to run down my cheek in a slow trickle. The pain in my head was nothing at the moment, I'd blocked it out. I was pissed and this woman had pissed me off twice in as many days.

It was her... the surly waitress. I turned back to her; my fists clenched. I leaned back, and even on wobbly legs I swung. Her head spun from the blow to her eye, and she fell to the ground grasping the side of her face. The blubberous man from the store came thundering to her defense; stopping dead in his tracks when his eyes met the open ends of both of our guns. Each of us had drawn and stood ready.

The woman scrambled backward in a crab walk to the curb, where the man helped her up. They stood cursing us even as we drove away.

I had a hard time finding my voice and squeaked out. "Do we have to go to the hospital?"

"You need stitches and to have it checked. If the crowd is bad at the hospital, we'll look into something else, OK? But let's get there and check first."

Before we even got to the emergency entrance, the chaos spilled out into the street. There would be no stitches at the hospital today.

"Let me think for a minute." he said. Then his eyebrows went up and he jammed the truck in drive.

A few minutes later we were in a quiet area of stores and offices. I was confused and looked at him. He smiled and pointed to a small building on the far side of the parking lot.

"The vet?" My revulsion obvious

"Why not?"

"But..." My voice hitched looking for words to express my objection but had none.

"Why not? He's cool and one of the friends we will be chatting with later tonight at the meeting."

"I just..." Again, I had no words.

He led me to the entry, and I was somehow repulsed by the thought. *A veterinarian?* I thought.

He must have seen the expression of revulsion on my face. Once inside he sat me in a chair and went to speak to the receptionist. A few moments later a man emerged, he was late forties-early fifties and cue ball bald. He smiled and they shook hands. Moments later we were seated in a small room with a metal table for the animal examinations. He came in holding a silver tray and making small talk as he laid out and prepared the things he'd need for the stitches. He couldn't have been from around here; he had a bit of a drawl to his words. "Are you going to the meeting tonight?"

We nodded.

"I'll be closing up shop early. Do you think you could take some supplies to the barn in your truck? I only have the Benz and it would sure be a help."

"No problem."

"When we're finished here, I'll have you pull round to the back of the building and we can load up."

"Now how about we have a peek at your noggin?" He approached and had me follow him over to the counter. He dragged my chair over next to me and half giggled tossing a wink in Mal's direction. "Sorry about the accommodations, we don't get too many of your kind in here."

I laughed but regretted it in a nanosecond and squinted; it made my head hurt. He caught this, nodded to Mal, and approached to remove the bandage. I flinched.

"Don't worry, I won't touch it yet, I only want to have a look at it."

He began to cut the tape to remove the gauze. It was stuck to my hair and pulled when he lifted it. I sucked a breath through my teeth and scrunched my face at the pain. He stopped and took my hand, placing it on the gauze to hold it in place. "I'll be right back."

He returned a moment later with a long syringe. I said nothing but must have looked terrified because he laughed and said, "This won't hurt a bit." Then he moved toward me and I leaned away from it. I swear the thing was three inches long, there was no way I was going to let him near me with that!

"Relax," he said.

"But..." I protested.

"I'm not going to use it as an injection but more like a topical with small pricks to the skin to numb it up a little so we can take the bandage off and get a good look."

I relaxed slightly and lifted my hand from the bandage, still flinching; it was amazing how much more it had begun to throb since his first attempt at removing the bandage. He lifted it once again and I felt a cool sensation followed by burning. Again, I sucked air across my teeth, resisting the urge to reach up and slap his hands away.

The blood had dried on the bandage, clinging to some of the hairs, and each time he moved the bandage it tugged at the wound. The small pricks and pulls were more painful than just ripping it off. I was over it by this point. "Oh, for God's sake, cut the damn hair!"

"I will have to shave a portion of your hair to stitch this up. You have quite the gash." He looked across the room to Mal.

"It was a can. From a skirmish at the grocery store."

He paused what he was doing and looked intently first to Mal and then back to me. "Right, then let's finish this up and send you on your way."

It took only a few minutes for him to clean the area and shave a small swath of hair along the half-moon gash in my head. He'd numbed the entire left side of my head from my ear to my neck and over the top. There was a strange sensation of some tugging but no pain as he placed the stitches with absolute precision. He bandaged the area and wrapped a gauze headband around my head. Mal gave me his beanie to wear over it.

We pulled the truck around to the rear of the building and they began loading totes into the bed of the truck. Also, animal traps and various bags and boxes. When they were finished, he came around to the passenger window and motioned for me to roll it down, while Mal climbed into the driver's seat. He handed me a small bottle of pills.

"For the pain." Then another much larger one with a label affixed to it saying, *3x daily.* "For infection," he said. "Take these three times a day for ten days. Then save the rest. There are enough antibiotics here for five courses."

We thanked him and said we'd see him tonight and pulled out of the parking lot, headed for home. Again, the drive was uneventful, almost surreal; a stark difference from what we saw in town, we made it home in no time. It was almost like the troubles were isolated to the city center, with no real effects being seen in the rural areas. We could tell Chris was off doing things as well when we went by the closed store that we'd had lunch in. There were effects, they were more subtle but still there. We both knew there would be more to come.

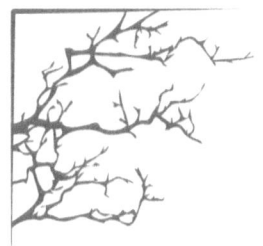

The meeting

It was only six o'clock, but by that time it was starting to get dark outside. To make the meeting look less like a meeting, it was decided that it was to be an Election Day barn cookout. We'd each brought a covered dish. A sign was affixed to the entrance of the barn.

Leave the politics at the door!

This was for the people who were not invited to the meeting but would unwittingly lend to its obscurity. When we arrived we shared hugs and handshakes. I took the dish over to the table where the others sat lined up. Various casseroles and pastas in different serving bowls of varied shapes and sizes filled the tables. The grill was roaring, and grease dripped from searing steaks, chicken, and burgers. The smell was mouthwatering and the mood... festive. What a complete change it was from the events of earlier.

This would change.

It took less than an hour before the topic shifted to the current election. Some talked about who voted, speculating about how people voted and who didn't vote. The disdain was palpable and difficult to ignore. An older man got up on a chair and began to shout for everyone to listen.

"Ladies and gentlemen, did you note the sign on the door? You were to leave the politics outside, away from this place. This gathering was organized to remind us that no matter the political arena, that we are first and foremost... a community."

A lady shouted in agreement.

"The food is about ready, so what do you say we agree to leave the politics outside and enjoy a meal with our neighbors?"

The sentiment was obscured somewhere in the mix, but the community was no longer a community as one might have seen so many years back when the old store was first established. Bygone were the days when horse and buggy would pull up and neighbors would chew the fat, so to speak. Yes, those days were gone, and we would soon find out how far gone.

The meal was good, with offerings of many different dishes. Most of the women exchanged recipes while the men gathered in groups. A few sat off from the rest with fierce anger and resentment in their eyes. These were the ones that were talking politics so heatedly earlier.

Because my head hurt, and I wasn't much for moving around, I sat observing the atmosphere. At one point I looked around and found that that Mal was missing, along with Chris, the store owner, and the two friends we shot with earlier in the day. Worry shrouded my mood until they all came strolling in the door like normal and Mal nodded my way.

A woman I'd never seen before approached me. "Are there many of these gatherings here?"

I was not paying attention and didn't understand the question. I turned and looked at her, "Hua?"

Her eyebrows raised. "I'm sorry, did I bother you?"

"Oh... No, I was watching everyone and didn't hear you." I twisted myself to face her and concentrate on the conversation, in spite of the fact that I could not seem to gather my thoughts in one place.

"I wondered if y'all often had many of these gatherings?"

I laughed, "Y'all? You ain't from around here are you?"

"No, we've only been here for about a month. We bought the old Robert's farm."

I righted myself and extended a hand to her, "Hi I'm Dani, well... Danielle, but people call me Dani."

"Pleased to meet you."

But before I could catch her name a man came over and gruffly grabbed her arm and the two left without another word.

The mood had changed in the barn, the lines having been drawn; so much for politics being left at the door. It seemed like it was the only thing that mattered to many of these people, they were unable to leave the issues outside.

Mal came over to where I was sitting and sat down. "How's it going?"

"Like watching a pot of spaghetti getting ready to boil over. You see the small bubbles bursting in the pot as it rises towards the rim. If it isn't turned down, it will spill over the sides and make a mess," I said.

He raised his eyebrows and looked about the room. Seeing things from my perspective offered a keen view. "We were so busy getting the stuff from the back of the truck and getting maps out to the guys that I'd failed to take note of how volatile this group had become."

The question, accetuated by the higher pitch in my voice highlighted my confusion with things that they'd been doing. "Maps?"

"Yea, we have one too. I'll show you when we get home, we can talk about them then."

"Ok, when are we leaving? This is looking a little reminiscent of the grocery store and making my head throb." I half-laughed and half-choked. Last thing I wanted was another can to the head.

"Let me go over and chat for five minutes and then we'll head out. Sound ok?"

"Sure, I'll be right here. Can't miss me; I'll be the girl with the white headband."

He smirked at me and got up. He took a few moments to scan the room, then wandered over to the others and made an animated gesture of explaining that I wasn't feeling well. The others did the same with their sympathies and I found it not only odd but annoying.

He gathered up our covered dish and came back to where I was sitting and offered me a hand up. He glanced in either direction with his eyes only and gave his chin an upward nod. I caught the vibe and reached out for his hand and rose.

Once we were outside, I began to question him. "What the...?"

He nudged me forward and shot me a look and a subtle, all but invisible nod that said no. I tried to make it seem like I'd forgotten something, fishing through my pockets.

"Ahhh, found it." I pulled the top off my Burt's Bees and began to slather it across my lips before jamming the cover back on and chatting as though it would have been a tragedy to have lost it. "I can't believe how many of these I've lost in like a week..." I yammered on as though I didn't have a care in the world but this damn tube of chapstick. "I thought I'd lost this one and I only opened it this afternoon. Ugh, I swear I need to buy these by the case." I crammed the stick of lip balm back into my pocket and smacked my lips, climbing into the truck.

Once we'd left and were on our way home, he began to explain. "There was a group of guys who showed up itching for a fight."

I looked at him, I couldn't understand why he and the others wouldn't shut them down. But before I could speak, he cut me off. "They weren't from around here. Something was off. Two of them were talking to someone on the phone around the side of the building. They said we were a difficult bunch and asked what else they could do to trigger people. We were unloading the truck on the other side of the garage and could hear. We listened and decided it was time for our friends to make a hasty exit. I couldn't say so when I sat down and needed to make a reason for us to leave expediently."

"I don't understand, why us? Why here? Wouldn't a riot be better in a city?"

"I know we're a small town, but also home to one of the area's largest gun clubs. I think it may have something to do with that; that's all we can figure."

I was a little uncomfortable with the thought of such things. "Do you think they were behind the scenes at the grocery store?" I looked at him, "Were they doing it all over? Who exactly are *THEY*?"

He looked at me and his eyes said all that needed saying, this would grow far worse... and fast. I was ready to be home, safe and warm, and for this day to be over. We drove home in silence, each in our own thoughts. Snowflakes littered the roadway as they accumulated one on top of another. Their crystalline shapes interlocking and creating a white blanket across the landscape. Winter was here.

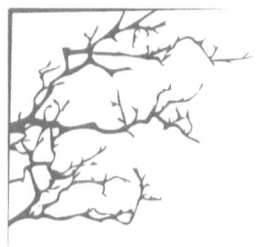

The Results

We relaxed and turned on the news to gain some perspective on the election. With eight candidates, the news was as expected, the polls were all over the place with no clear leader. The fabric of our election system had been tattered, with little hope that our fate would be decided by tonight. One of the candidates was calling for recounts and the election wasn't even over.

Another candidate campaigned heavy inside the cities, targeting the inner-city poor with promises of more government assistance, he wanted the electoral college vote thrown out. While another targeted the Midwestern farm states, crying out that the popular vote was corrupted by illegal and fraudulent voting and therefore the only true way to decide was with the votes of the electoral college. Causes flung into the mix from every direction, some said 'this is not fair' while others shouted from podiums 'that is discrimination'. The issues were nothing more than talking points for the talking heads. Term limits, flat tax, immigration... all tossed in the mix of ways to convert an outraged voter. One was socialist and another communist. "*We are a democracy!*" cried one across a loudspeaker, while another scoffed at the mob rule mentality of democracy, reminding them all, "*We are a constitutional republic and not a democracy.*" All of it, a smokescreen, to shroud the cloud of war which was hanging in the air.

We'd witnessed the circus, and it was not at all entertaining. So many; pandering for the masses, no real progress made. Only upheaval and angst. The people fighting amongst themselves; distractions and mayhem. It was no longer about the election; all the bickering and screaming had come to a head and nothing would stop what was coming. Nothing!

The slide into chaos and anarchy had begun, there would be no stopping it; all we could do was hope and try to survive it. That's what the others were doing, preparing for the fight. Gathering and organizing supplies, setting up communication and rendezvous points. Preparing for the fight that was on the doorstep, in every city, town, and neighborhood.

We sat quiet and watched the chaos in the bigger cities, L.A., Atlanta, New York, and even Boston had riots and destruction where rioters, turned looters, had set fire to cars and buildings. Police in riot gear were firing rubber bullets at the masses of people who were smashing windows and stealing whatever was at hand. Flip the channel again to a scene where some less than easy going folks were turning over a car, in the background a young woman stood with blood running into her eyes. She was swiping at it with blood-soaked hands and sobbing. No one was helping her as she stood bleeding in the night.

I held his arm; I was fearful of what was to come. "Are you kidding me? What is wrong with people?"

"I don't know, babe." he said and kissed the top of my head.

"Now you know why I didn't want you going into Boston this week."

I nodded, my eyes tracing the stern look on his face, a shudder jerked me into the stark knowledge that it could have saved my life. "Thank God, one of us had some sense. I could've been in the middle of all that."

"I was hoping I was wrong, but I felt like this one wasn't going to go down easy, and we needed to step back and eyeball things for a bit. We don't even know what we are preparing for."

"Mal, this is scaring me. What do you think will happen?"

"We've been talking about it for a while now and there's no way to know Dani."

"Well, how do we know anything will happen?"

"We don't. Best case scenario? Nothing more than what we have seen up to now."

The bile rose in my throat and I gulped it down. "And worst?"

"Worst?" He raised his eyebrows and turned toward me. "Civil war."

"Like the north and south?"

"Yes, but none like we have ever known. Same as the voting today... It could be the neighbor, the little old lady, or the waitress that is against us. It could be anyone and as we know people don't have the same kind of community engagement they once had. There will be no clear lines. Unlike the south and north in the first civil war where blue and gray uniforms told who was on which side, we don't know what will happen."

"Not the old lady."

He laughed, "No, probably not her."

I hopped up from the sofa and snatched my purse off the table. I dug around in the bottom of it and began tossing things out onto the table.

"What the heck are you doing Dani?"

"Looking for her number."

"That'll be a while, that thing is a bottomless pit," he laughed.

I flashed him a side eye glare then rolled my eyes and dumped the purse onto the table. "Here it is," I cried out triumphant, holding up a small card. Raising my eyebrows in smug satisfaction I grabbed my phone and dialed the number.

Ring... Ring...

On the third ring she answered. The small voice shaky on the other end. "Hello."

"Hello," I responded a little too quickly. "I don't know if you'll remember me. Pancakes?" I offered.

She laughed a little, "Yes, yes I do. How are you?"

"I'm good, I was wondering how you were doing."

"I'm doing ok, I wish I would have gone to the store, but after voting I was so shaken up that I just wanted to come straight home."

"Well, you didn't need to be in town today anyway. Do you need anything? We could stop by tomorrow."

"I could use some coffee. I just realized I'm almost out."

"No problem, we'll bring you some in the morning. Can I have your address?"

She gave me her address and I said we would pop in on her in the morning. After I hung up the phone, I turned to Mal. "We'll go tomorrow morning with some coffee; She said she'd sure love some."

He smiled and nodded.

It had been a long day and all I wanted was a hot bath. My head couldn't get wet for at least a few days, so a hot bath was just what the doctor ordered. I added some lavender and Epsom salts to help release the tension, grabbed a glass of wine, and the latest issue of Better Homes and Gardens magazine to have a look at the next dynamite project I'd inevitably whine at Mal to do.

He caught a glimpse of me as I headed for the bathtub, magazine under my arm and wine in hand. "Dang it! I meant to burn that before you saw it."

I glared at him. He winked and smiled.

He continued to sit in front of the election coverage for a while after I'd gone to the bedroom, climbed into bed and opted for an old favorite chick flick. My head hurt and I was exhausted from the day, I simply wanted a little bit of the good ole creature comforts and to be free from the chaos of the election.

It Begins

I must have fallen asleep; the room was dark and Mal lay snoring beside me. Something felt off, I couldn't put my finger on it, but it was something. It was dark, too dark; the nightlight in the bathroom was out. I raised my head and looked to where the red digits of the clock should be to find nothing. The power was out, that's all. I started to push myself up to sit but Mal's arm pushed me down. He wasn't asleep! Something was wrong!

His hot breath brushed my cheek he was so close, he whispered, the sounds hushed in my ear. "Roll over, then slide off the bed onto the floor and crawl under. Remember, the shotgun is near the head of the bed. Take the safety off... but be quiet."

I began to object, and he pressed on my chest. "Someone is rummaging in the living room; now get under the bed."

I did as he instructed and rolled out of bed and onto the floor. I shimmied up underneath and felt around until my hand found the shotgun. We kept my 12 gauge under the bed, and I was quite familiar with it. The cold metal of the barrel was stark, and I ran my hand along the smooth cold steal in search of the safety. It was right where I knew it would be and I shifted it to the fire position, taking care to make it quiet.

Mal didn't move until after I was under the bed. He must have been listening for the sound of the safety disengaging. He too, now rolled to the far side of the bed and crouched behind leaning against the mattress for cover. The moonlight came through the curtains and my eyes had adjusted so that I could see much of the doorway and into the hallway.

Glancing behind me I saw Mal's legs below the bed, in front of him held at knee level, both hands on his Kimber .45. This was the one he kept bedside; it looked a lot like his 9mm but a little more substantial. The pounding in my chest sounded so loud in my ears, I swore it echoed through the woods and into the next town over. I strained to peer further into the hallway. A low raspy wheeze came first, followed by a humongous mass obscuring the light. As his body came into view, I could see the first man, he was a considerable man, overweight; but what I saw behind him was at first shocking. Perhaps the lighting was off, but the second one was voluminous, much heftier than the first.

He wheezed to another man standing behind him, "I know they have guns; he must, he belongs to the gun club. Shut up and look for them."

The second man whined, "They're all locked in the safe out in the hallway."

"No, they're not, they never are. These people are all paranoid. Check behind the doors."

"I don't wanna do this, I'm outta here." The second man said and waddled from view.

"Get back here," the old fat man wheezed. "I ain't gonna protect you when he wakes up."

"He's awake." Mal's voice boomed in the silence.

The man stood rigid in the doorway and raised a long gun, unable to focus on where Mal was, he waved it back and forth. "Get on out here, let's get this party started." His voice rasped.

Although the gun was loaded and a round chambered, Mal pulled the slide back to make the sound of a round chambering in hopes it might dissuade this intruder.

It didn't.

"I hear ya." He took a step into the room.

I was laying on my side, shotgun aimed at the giant midsection jiggling when he moved. I would not miss.

He lifted the gun and fired it into the room, missing the area where Mal remained crouched, but only by a fraction. Mal fired back at him over the bed, he had no clear view of the man, but must have been firing in the direction of the muzzle flash.

I could see him, he stood not ten feet from me. The man stumbled and fired again. Twice he shot in Mal's direction pinning him behind the bed as he took aim over and over.

He took a step towards where Mal was and if he took any more, I'd lose my shot. The man fired again, and so did I. Pulling the trigger, a deafening sound emerged from the gun and echoed under the bed. The double ought buck raced from the end of the barrel, and my ears rang so loud I couldn't even hear the sound of the shell ejecting as I loaded the next round in pure instinct.

The man stumbled backward and fell into the hallway. A scream echoed from the other room; the other man had not left but was still rummaging around the living room. I fired again through the doorway into the hall although I couldn't see him. Again, I ejected the shell and loaded the next round.

Mal grabbed my foot. I glanced backward and saw him moving towards the doorway. Shotgun in hand I shimmied backward trying to squeeze out from under the bed, I couldn't go forward, that would put me in view of the hallway.

Once out from under the bed, I rose onto my knees, shotgun splayed over the bed covering Mal as he cleared the hallway and then the house. I was frozen staring at the man laying half in and half out of the bedroom. He never moved, I half expected him to, or perhaps hoped. I didn't want to kill him.

My eyes began to sting as the tears burned their way through to the surface. The first one lingered on the bottom lash of my right eye before falling and with that single tear, all of them emerged in a stream down both cheeks. I'd never even killed a squirrel... anything... Ever. I was frozen where I knelt, gun aimed to the hallway, staring at the body. Horrified, but also not. Once the tears subsided, my mind cleared. I reached over to the bedside table and grabbed my cell phone and carefully punched the numbers, 9-1-1. I listened but nothing happened. I held the phone out at arm's length, no signal, not even a single bar of service.

Mal returned to the bedroom and took the shotgun from my hands sitting me in the chair across the room. I could no longer see the man.

"Stay here for a few minutes, I'll be right back."

I nodded and continued to look at my cell phone. My head hurt, the throbbing resounding with every beat of my heart. I was struggling to come to grips with what had happened, trying to reconcile the events. Deep down my mind told me it was only the beginning.

I felt like I'd been sitting in the corner forever while Mal shuffled around in the other room. My mind could not forget the image of the dead man. Running in circles around the events; did I have to kill him? Was there any other way? I felt like I was going crazy, replaying the moment over and over. Mal came for me and we went into the living room where he'd stoked the fire and had a pot on for coffee.

I began to sob again; anger, fear, anguish, guilt, and every other emotion overtook me all at once. Sobbing, I cried, "How dare these men come into our home? Who were they? And Why? Oh right, for the guns. They wanted to steal our guns?"

The questions and comments were more of a means for my mind to grasp what had happened than anything else. I had so many questions. I sat down aloof, engrossed in my thoughts; fidgeting in front of the stove, running again all through the steps of what happened. I was so wrapped up in it that I'd forgotten to ask him how the election went.

"Mal, what happened with the election?" I looked at him.

"What didn't?"

"What's that supposed to mean?"

He shook his head and sighed. "The polls were all over the place. First one party was in the lead, then another. With so many candidates the results may not be known for months." He scratched his head and took a seat next to me. "The candidate from Alaska conceded and the state has filed papers for Secession. Texas followed, along with a separatist movement to make Colorado, Wyoming, Utah, and Montana its own country. The candidate from California demanded a recount before the voting was even finished."

"All of this happened after I went to bed?"

"Yea, around ten o'clock things began to get dicey when the two women candidates filed against one of the other candidates for sexual harassment. The news was all downhill from there."

"So, who's the President?"

"I don't think anyone knows. There's no clear winner. At this point, I don't think it matters who." He stood and went to the coffee perking on the wood stove. He poured each of us a cup, came back, and sat down.

Silence fell between us for a time. It was still dark, but that didn't mean anything in the cold months. It could be midnight or six in the morning.

I wondered, "What time is it?"

He glanced at his watch. "Five forty-five."

"Oh."

We both looked back to our coffees. I wondered what the next days or weeks would hold.

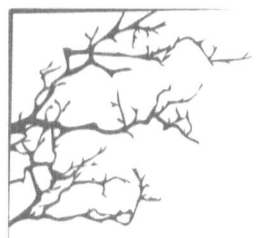

Day One

I NEVER MINDED COOKING breakfast, but on the wood stove, it almost seemed like fun. Mal headed to town to find the police and file a report about the home invasion. We both had seen the TV shows that said not to move the body, but we had to move the body out of the house. Mal wanted to go right away, but I wouldn't stay home alone, and we were both afraid to leave the house open.

I knew it was a chicken-shit move, but I was terrified to go for the police. I know I had the right to shoot, he was firing at us. I was still scared. I'd heard tales of burglaries gone wrong and the perp being shot, then the family coming back and suing the homeowner. Worse yet, the homeowner being arrested. The whole thing baffled me, if the person had not been committing a crime they never would have been shot. It was terrifying for me. Once the sun came up, I felt better and so did Mal. It was only a ten-minute drive to the police station; they should be back any minute.

I was still in my robe, because I didn't want to go back into the bedroom for clothes until the police came. More coffee was made; some bacon, potatoes, and eggs sat warming on the wood stove. The time seemed to tick slower and slower. My nerves were shot, and I couldn't help but pace.

My thoughts became words. "What if they want to arrest me?" My hands wringing, I fidgeted on the seat. "Oh, be quiet, they're not going to arrest you... Dammit!" I stomped off to the bedroom careful not to disturb anything and grabbed my jeans and a hoodie. "Screw this! That asshole was shooting at us. I had every right to protect myself!"

After I dressed, I returned to the stove and added some wood. Something was wrong, it's been too long. I began to worry about Mal. How selfish I'd been to only worry about myself. What if something happened to him? There are some crazies active in the area and the world was getting more unstable by the minute.

As I began my second lap around the living room, cursing and talking to myself, tires crunched on the gravel driveway. My heart leapt into my throat and I ran for the window to look. It was Mal!

The door flung open and I raced out clinging to him before he could even say anything.

"What took you so long?" I blurted out and tipped my head to the side looking around him. "Where's the police?"

"They'll be here. Let's go inside." His eyes shifted around the yard before he grabbed the door handle.

"What's wrong?"

"I went in to file a report and told them what happened. I was shocked to find dozens of cops and the cells were full down at the station. After I told them what happened, they were not surprised. The sheriff said violence had broken out all across the country."

I sat shocked beside him and waited for more.

"If this fat bastard is who they think he is, he's got two boys. The fat one that was with him last night, and another. The fat boy is kinda dumb and lazy... so I'm not so worried about him, but the other one? They've had issues with him before and he might be a problem. May even come looking for some revenge. He has a history of violence."

"What should we do?" The crack in my voice sounding more like pleading than a question.

"The police will be here in a little while; they have some other stuff to look into first. The officer said to sit tight and try not to touch anything. I told him we moved the body out the back door. He wasn't too happy about it but said we shouldn't worry."

"Pfffft... Worry? Who's worried?"

He tipped his head and raised an eyebrow looking at me like I'd lost a few marbles. "Hua?" He smirked shaking his head.

"I was popping off. Being contrary is all. I needed a little bit of humor."

"Humor?"

"Yea, the country is in chaos, half of it wants war while the other half wants to fight over politics and bring about anarchy, a dead guy is on the back porch with two sons that will now want to kill us, and they say don't worry."

He laughed an uneasy laugh and nodded.

"But hey on the bright side... breakfast is ready!"

The troubled look on his face was stressing me out. He was trying to make me feel better, but he couldn't hide his concern. I was aware like he was what this all meant, and I expected it was gonna get a whole lot worse. We ate in silence, each in our own thoughts.

It took a good hour before the sheriff arrived. Stepping over the body, he gave an off handed nod at the man. "Just as I thought," he said nodding his head and looking around. "Are the boys here too?"

"Uh... no. What boys?" I was not expecting that there would be more.

"The other one got away, there were only two of them that we saw last night," Mal explained.

"I see," he shrugged and started writing in his small pad. "And what time did all this take place?"

"Uh... I'm not sure. The power was out so the clocks weren't showing time. But when I put my watch on it was a little before four and by then, we'd moved him out of the room and taken some time to clear the house and calm down."

"So, about three in the morning, sound good?" The sheriff said never looking up from his pen.

"Yea, that might be close."

"We know these guys. They are a plague on the town," he said, continuing to write.

After he finished writing he looked up and glanced between us. He offered me a reassuring smile. "Now you said there was one other here?"

"Yes," I spouted. "He was bigger than the guy outside."

"Hummm..."

Mal and I looked at one another, curious as to the blasé tone the sheriff had. It was almost as though he didn't care that the man was dead. After a few moments of searching through his phone he showed us a photo of a man. He looked similar to the man on the porch and asked us if we recognized him. We both shook our heads side to side. He then swiped the phone and showed us another.

I gasped and looked horrified to Mal. "That's him."

"Him?" The sherrif raised one eyebrow and tilted his head toward the photo.

"He was at the grocery store, we believe he is the one who gave me this," I said pointing the bandage on my head.

"I was going to ask you about that. What happened?"

"Yesterday in town, we went for a few things and all hell broke loose right in the store!" The words came out agitated trying to convey the mayhem we'd seen.

The sheriff nodded writing on his small pad. "Uh hua."

Mal finished the tale for him. "Someone hit her on the head with a can, the guy at the store thought it was a can of peas, but we aren't sure."

The sheriff looked up, "Peas you say." He looked at us with the side of his mouth upturned in a slight smirk.

"We aren't sure but, that man, in the picture? He was in the aisle, right behind me when it started,"

"After the incident, when we were leaving the store, he was with that surly waitress from the diner and she pulled my hair. Wow... did that hurt, and the blood was in my eyes. I punched her lights out."

"I see." The Sheriff listened to our account of the incident at the store. Unaffected or surprised at what we'd said.

I was nervous, now I'd shot someone and assaulted the waitress. I sat on the chair, tears welling up in my eyes. "How could everything have gone so wrong?" I put my face in my hands and Mal came over and put his hand on my back.

"All of it will be alright. Nothing you've done is going to come back on you. These two are nothing but trouble."

Mal stepped up beside me putting his arm around my shoulder. "Do you think there will be more trouble?"

"Can't say, but I'd make sure to lock up tight, things have gone downhill since yesterday and I expect worse yet."

A van pulled into the driveway and two men got out with a stretcher to fetch the body. The sheriff took pictures inside the house and outside noting bullet holes and where we said we were when the burglary was happening. He found multiple holes in the bedroom wall near where Mal had been crouched behind the bed and shell casings in the hallway. The gun that we dared not touch was still laying on the floor in the hallway where the sheriff retrieved it and bagged it up as evidence.

He hemmed and hawed about our guns that were used in the shootout saying, "I'm supposed to take these for evidence but with everything going on I also don't want to leave you defenseless. Let me call this in and find out what the county prosecutor thinks, but this is pretty clear cut to me, and I doubt you'll need to worry about it," he said. "I'd say call a lawyer just to be safe, but the phones aren't working. We won't be investigating this until after things settle down and you will have a chance to contact one, so sit tight and stay safe."

The sheriff spoke to Mal outside for a few moments before pulling away with the van following him. My anxiety subsided some over the shooting incident, but I was still on edge about his sons and the state of the country right now.

Plans I cleaned things up, but the hallway was a mess and it made me sick to my stomach. I never would have thought with all the shooting we'd done, that it would feel like it did to shoot at a person, much less kill them. The adrenaline was pumping, I never paused to even think about it. I'd fired and down he fell. The morning was full of trepidation and angst, still unsure of how the incident would turn out as I tried to clean up the mess and decide if anything had been taken.

Mal shouted from the other room, "Babe! Some of the guys are here, can you toss on a pot?"

"Oh sure, I'm cleaning blood and guts off the wall, but hey... let me stop and make a pot of coffee real quick." I stood up, stomping toward the kitchen.

He looked at me, "You OK?"

"Not at all. Just ignore me. I think I'm still a little freaked out is all. I'm sorry I snapped at you," I said making my way over to him and stretching onto my tippy toes to give him a quick kiss on the cheek. I was sorry; I don't even know why I snapped like that. It wasn't like I was enjoying cleaning up all of the blood splatter on the hallway wall.

"Dammit, why didn't I use the 9mm? It would have left less of a mess." For some reason this struck me as funny, I giggled while setting the pot on the wood stove and adding a couple sticks of wood.

Mal entered the room as I laughed. "What's so funny?"

"Nothing, the thought was kind of morbid," I said shaking my head and going back into the kitchen.

"Hey," I called from the kitchen. "Anyone up for a *sammich*," I snickered, peering at them, and winking from around the corner.

They all laughed and agreed it was getting to be lunch time. I whipped up some tuna salad and grabbed a bag of chips, some pickles, left-over macaroni salad, and headed for the dining room where they were all seated around the table. I laid out the sandwiches and other foods and went for beers before returning and sliding into the seat next to Mal. "So, what's going on?" I plopped down taking a giant swig from my beer.

"Mal was filling us in on your intruders last night," the friendly neighborhood vet said. "How's your head?"

"The shootout didn't do much for my headache, but OK I think." I reached for the bandage, "I should change this though."

"I'll give it a check after we eat," he said.

"What's your name, doc?"

"Oh right...Pleasure to meet you, I'm Mike, Mike Ezio."

I'd met the others seated around the table from the gun club earlier. Chris came, he owned the store we ate at yesterday, he was married to Jen and they had two teenage boys. Then at the end of the table was Joe. I thought Mal was tall, but Joe was six foot eight, a burly man who always wore a beanie hat and flannel shirt. And beside him was Steve, I was good friends with his wife Pam, they often came shooting with us along with Meeker and his wife Fawn. The guys called him Meeker for reasons unknown to me but had something to do with his name and some nighttime stunt they pulled when they were teenagers. They had three small children all under age ten.

Only the guys came to chat, but we planned to get together later in the afternoon with the ladies as well to do something they all called recon for the OP. The talk all had the sound of military lingo, and I was over it by then. Mal would fill me in on anything I needed to know later.

I excused myself, got up, and grabbed the dishes. Not wanting to deal with it I began clearing things from the table. The beer was not even close to tasty for me and I decided a hot cup of cocoa was a much better idea. The kettle was on the stove and hot, so I curled up in the living room with my latest read and sipped the hot chocolate, pondering what everything meant now.

When the others left, I reminded Mal that we were going to bring the old lady some coffee. I'd forgotten amid all the chaos about her coffee and was anxious to check on her. I was worried about her all alone after the events of last night. We gathered up some coffee and other things to take up to her and headed out the door.

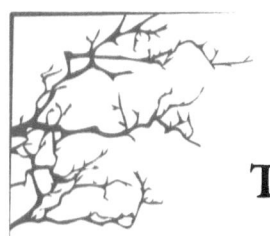

The Old Woman

She lived at the top of the hillside that looked down over the town in an old New Englander house that her family built in the 1700's. It wasn't that far from where we were, so we decided to take the path through the woods, up the steep incline to the tree line that bordered her pasture. The woods were quiet, and the view of the area, panoramic. The brisk November morning was colder than it had been all season and the crisp smell of snow hung in the air. My cellphone had bars again, so I phoned ahead to say we were coming and not to shoot us coming across the pasture. We made it to the farmhouse in less than thirty minutes where she greeted us with some hot tea. I wasn't sure what she'd put into the tea, but it was delicious with a hint of mint and honey.

"I'm sorry I couldn't offer you a good cuppa jo, but I ran out yesterday."

"That's right," I smiled at her, reaching for my pack. I reached in and pulled a pound of Black Rifle coffee from the pouch and handed it to her.

"Oh, this is too much Dani."

"Nahh, we got lots of it," Mal shoved the bag in her direction. "I ordered it online and built up a nice stash."

Tossing a side eyed wink at Mal. "Yes, because it is after all about the coffee, you see."

The old lady smiled and thanked us for the coffee and went to the kitchen to put it in the cupboard. The house was chilly, not just chilly but downright cold. Mal got up and went over to check the wood stove which had burned down to tiny embers. "Do you heat with the stove?"

"Yes, I haven't been able to pull the wood in from the barn yet today."

"You have to go to the barn each day for the wood?" He frowned and appeared almost cross.

"Yes," she hung her head. "My son comes and loads the shed outside the door each month, but we had words last time he was here about the election and he told me I could do my own wood. I thought it would blow over, but two months have passed now, and he hasn't answered his phone or been by to visit."

Mal grew angry, his face red. "Where's the wood," he shouted at her.

"Mal," I said, reaching for his arm with a pleading look.

His look softened and he spoke to her again in a much kinder tone. "Where's the wood? I'll bring enough for the night and then ask the guys to come by tomorrow to fill your shed."

"But..."

"No buts," I interjected. "He's a guy and they seem to have this innate need to save the damsel in distress. You wouldn't want to take away his ego moment and not let him save you, would you?"

She rose and went over to Mal and smiled at him. "Then I will bake something for you."

He smiled and headed out the door, while I followed her to the kitchen. When I pulled off my hat, her hands went to her mouth.

"What on earth happened to you?" She yelled, pointing to the bandage wrapped around my head.

"Oh, that's right," I said reaching for the bandage. "It happened after we saw you at the polling station." I moved over toward the counter. "We went to the store after leaving you. It ended up being a mini riot in the middle of the grocery store, and someone hit me in the head with a can. The store manager was at least somewhat sure I got beaned with some peas." A tiny giggle and she got it, smiling at me.

"Are you OK?" She paused the swift pouring of this, adding that to the recipe. The concern on her face chiseled in the lines across her forehead.

"Yea, it hurts where the stitches are, but otherwise I feel fine."

"People are so rude these days." She returned to her mixing. I was fascinated with how fast she expertly added just the right amount of ingredients without so much as a scoop or spoon to measure.

"Listen..." I turned to face her giving her a grave look. "Mal and I will come back tomorrow, but it might be best if you came with us for a little while. We are only at the bottom of the hill and we have a spare bedroom. We can come up and feed the stove to keep it warm, but I am worried you may not be safe here alone."

"No, I couldn't. I've lived here all my life. I'm not leaving."

The old woman stood firm her small bony fingers curled into small fists on her hips. Somehow, I figured she wouldn't but at least she'd know that if necessary, she had a place for her to go.

"Well don't be going into the grocery store without us, OK?" I warned. "I don't think it will be safe for a few days until all this blows over."

She nodded in agreement and shoved the first sheet of chocolate chip cookies into the oven in record time. I liked her, I did very much so, she reminded me of my own grandmother, and I worried for her. I hadn't told her about the break-in at our house because I didn't want to scare her. We didn't know what happened to the other guy and if they would break into our house knowing we were armed; she would surely be an easy target for them.

Mal filled the entire side entry with wood and stacked enough inside by the wood stove to get her through the night. "There should be no reason for you to go out in the cold," he brushed off a few flakes from his jacket.

"It's snowing?"

"Yes, it started with some flurries a short time ago, but it is coming down hard now. We need to start on back." The look he had was troubled and I didn't know why. I opened my mouth to speak but he glared at me, his head moving almost imperceptibly from side to side. I turned and reached for my jacket my eyes pleading with her to come with us. She turned away and packed Mal's warm gooey cookies into a paper bag.

Mal took the bag from her, holding her hand longer than a passing shake. "You will need protection. I'd prefer you came with us, but we can't stay here now, our own home needs our attention. If I come back up later, might you stay the night with us?"

"I'll stay in my home," she said, resolute in her decision.

"OK, c'mon Malachi, we have a bit of a hike and it's going to be dark soon."

He held out his hand to her and grasped it. "Lock the doors. Do you have a gun?"

"I have my dad's old shotgun," she waved with pride at the antique hanging over the mantle.

"Well, that might be a bit much for personal protection," Mal said bending to his ankle and retrieving his small .380 that was always strapped to his ankle. "I'd feel better if you kept this."

"I don't think I can shoot that," she said. Her eyes the size of saucers, she pushed it back at him.

"I mean it," he said with more force.

I reached for his arm again. "I haven't told her about last night."

He looked from her to me and sighed, shaking his head.

Her eyes welled up and her face lost its light. "What happened last night?"

I looked down, "I didn't want to worry you, but Mal is right." I could see it pained him that he'd made the old lady cry with his forcefulness, but he was worried for her safety.

"Last night," I began and paused looking down. "Last night some unsavory types broke into our house and we had to defend ourselves."

Her eyes widened and she gasped, holding her tiny, crooked fingers up to cover her mouth.

"There are still a couple of these miscreants prowling the area and we only want you to be safe," I pleaded.

She smiled walked up to Mal and gave him a hug. "I will take the gun if you show me how it works, and I have your number if I have any problems."

Mal smiled at her and placed the small pistol in her hands. He rolled it over showing her where the safety was and how to load the bullets. She removed the magazine and showed him she could flip the safety off and then on. She didn't want to go outside and shoot it but assured us she'd shot her daddy's guns on more than one occasion.

By the time we went outside, an inch of snow lay on the ground. At least the walk was for the most part downhill. I didn't have my snow boots on, I was only wearing my tennis shoes and the snow was in one of my shoes.

"Well, this sucks!"

"What's wrong Dani?"

"I got snow up my pant leg and now in my shoe." I scowled in his direction before slipping on a patch of snow-covered leaves and sliding down a steep slope. A tree at the bottom of the incline stopped me, but none too gentle. By the time Mal reached me I was on my feet, shouting and cursing trying to shake the snow out from under my shirt.

Mal grabbed my mouth dragging me back to the ground. The look in his eyes told me once again that something was very wrong. I shrugged my shoulders, and he released my mouth. Eyes wide I tipped my head questioning what was up. He pointed to his eyes with his index and middle finger and then to an area into the woods.

I saw them. One was the fat man that I recognized from the store. Looking at him this way, he could have even been the one in our house last night. They were walking through the woods crashing through the brush in the direction of the town. We were sure that they hadn't seen us, but still waited for them to disappear into the trees before hurrying home.

Mal checked out the house and the small indicators he'd left that would tell us someone had been there. They were all precisely as he'd left them, the house was untouched.

Questions rose from both of us, wondering why these men were in the woods near here. Only our house, the old woman and a small camp that was now closed were in this area.

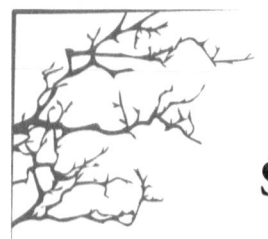

Securing Home

I tossed some burgers in a cast iron pan and set them to cooking on the wood stove while placing a couple of foil wrapped potatoes inside the door of the stove to bake. "Mal," I called out to him through the door. "Bring more wood when you come in."

The draft that blew through the entry was frigid and made me shiver. After closing the door, I grabbed the last few sticks of wood in the box, tossed them into the stove and stood warming myself up. I didn't plan to make any huge meals but was thinking about the length of time the power had been out and wondered if I needed to cook the food in the fridge before it went bad.

Mal came through the door with a full armload of wood that almost filled the wood box and went straight to the freezer and began tossing the contents into a grocery bag.

"What are you doing with that?"

"Grab a bag," he said, handing me another bag.

He filled them both and headed for the door. I followed and found that he'd pulled out the old truck box and chained it to the front porch.

"I think things are supposed to stay cold for a while," he said.

"What a fantastic idea." My excitement overtaking my mouth, I turned and hurried back for the rest of the contents.

Once we were done and inside warming up with our burgers Mal explained how he'd locked it all up and secured the barn.

"Do you think there will be trouble?"

"I don't know, but we still don't know what happened with the election, so there is bound to be more riots and unrest. Plus, I think we need to take extra precautions after last night."

I nodded, chomping on my food. He was right, we were not sure why the power was out, nor what happened with the election. The radio was on the shelf, I went and turned it on to find out if we could catch any news on what was happening with the election.

The newscaster spoke in solemn tones, *"While the results are still not clear, more than one candidate has demanded a recount. Cities are in chaos; Boston, New York, Denver, Los Angeles, and Portland are total losses, and the anarchy is spreading. There have been massive casualties in these areas and the violence is moving outward from the hot spots with rioting and random acts of violence. Please, my friends, remain in your homes this evening."*

It was horrifying to listen to the news describing so much violence, the small city of Keene was nothing compared to what was happening in the major cities. Voter fraud was epic while claims of vote suppression rang out in the background. Panic in the man's voice called out and the broadcast went dead. It was evident that this would not end well. I was immobilized for the moment, my mind spun with images from the store the day before.

Mal must have seen the look on my face. He came over and sat next to me wrapping his arm around me, "It'll be OK, I think we are safe here," he said in hushed tones to ease my nerves.

"It's not gonna be OK," I spat, jumping up from the sofa. "It's never gonna be OK."

I'd begun pacing the room, "Those people?" I said, pointing toward the radio. "Those are the same kind of people that were in the grocery store and we aren't safe. We saw that last night."

Mal stood and walked toward me but I was upset, really upset. "No, Malachi. You need to listen; I am not being irrational. I'm in fact very rational right now. We can't sit here and wait it out. We need to prepare, lock this place down. Hide some of the guns and set some alarm traps. Those assholes who came here? They'll be back."

"Alright, alright, calm down. We can't freak right now."

"Freak?" I was irrationally pissed about his response. "I am NOT freaking!"

"I know," he said. "Bad choice of words. What I mean is we should sit, be calm, and create a to-do list of everything we think we should do and go at it more organized is all."

"You're right, I'm sorry." I slouched into the chair; shoulders slumped from the anxiety that hung over me like a cloud. "Maybe I did freak for a moment."

He smiled at me and said, "You are right though, we need to take this serious. I don't know if they will return for a little payback, but I do know we were not as ready for them as I'd have liked to have been."

Worry echoed through him, from his furrowed brow to his tense posture. I'd made a valid point and now he too was concerned. This would have been his forte, I was more the easy-going limo driver who liked manicures and makeup. I was now faced with the hard realities of all those things he'd been talking about all these months. I liked shooting with him, funny that. He'd always said a high-heeled woman with a gun was the most dangerous critter on earth. I'd laughed it off pretending to be all badass, but in fact, I was a whole lot less badass and very helpless.

I was not prepared for any of this. Not physically, mentally, or emotionally. I was on the verge of a complete freak out and he was sitting there making a list. All I wanted to do was run from the house screaming at everyone to stop. The processes that made these people act this way was troubling to me. I mean, the surly waitress... I could see her acting badly like she had at the store, because she had acted badly before it all. But nothing had gone wrong yet, there was no declared winner. Yet normal people were acting out. There was no reason for this as far as I could tell.

I left it all hanging out there like a bad omen and wandered off to the bedroom for my warm fuzzies. Which is what Mal called my fuzzy pink bathrobe and slippers. It always made me feel better to snuggle down warm, with a hot cup of something, a book, and my warm fuzzies. I tried to read but my mind kept shifting to the people and the riots. All of this scared me, I wasn't sure I could handle it at all.

"Hey Dani," Mal called out. "You still with me?"

"Oh... What?" I looked up at him, a little confused. I'd gotten lost in my own thoughts and didn't even realize that he'd even now begun to secure the windows.

"Can you hand me that coffee can on the table? The one with the screws in it."

"Oh sure." I put the book down, I wasn't reading it anyway, and rose to join him in the kitchen.

I grabbed the can and walked to the window where he was securing a hinge to a piece of plywood laid out across the counter. "What is that for?" Unsure what a hinge had to do with things.

"A shutter," he smiled widely at me. "We can close them, and it will, with any luck, keep anyone from coming in the windows." I looked skeptical and he added, "But, we can still open them for the sunlight."

"Ohh..." I wasn't sure what I thought of it, all ugly and putting holes in my newly painted trim, but it was an ingenious idea. I began to envision them painted and started considering colors, wondering if I should offset it with an accent color or paint them the same as the trim. Anything to take my mind from the issues.

"Oh?" His voice startled me.

"I'm sorry," I said and smiled at him. "I was thinking about what color to paint them."

He laughed and hugged me, but I felt foolish. There I was, standing in front of the the window, worried about what color paint would look good; when they were meant to keep us from getting killed. The paint color seemed pretty stupid now.

"That's just like you," he chuckled. "Here, I am boarding up the windows and you're looking for a way to make it match. You always find a way to make things seem... not so bad."

Feeling sheepish, I gave a half-hearted giggle. "Yea, that's me... You save the world and I decorate it."

For some reason, the optimist in me was speaking a little less at the moment. What was there to be positive about after all? The world was crumbling around us and I was worried about the paint on the woodwork. I felt like one of those simpering fools and shoved past him to the kitchen. "Guess I'd better wash up these dishes."

Mal started toward me. "Aww Dani, I didn't mean to laugh at you. It's just that..." A loud banging on the door stopped him mid-sentence.

I hurried for the living room and the shotgun while Mal drew his gun and crept to look out the window and find out who it was. Peering onto the porch, he was on edge. Were he a cat, his back would have been hunched and tail puffed out, the tension was so evident. Once he caught sight of who it was, his shoulders relaxed.

"It's OK," he said. "Of course, it is Joe and he had to scare us practically to death."

The Riots Mal unbolted the door and Joe came in shaking off the cold and brushing the snow from his shoulders and hat. "Whew, the snow is really starting to come down out there."

"Hey Joe," Mal said taking his hat and coat.

Joe moseyed up to the fire, holding his hands out in front of it and rubbing them together to warm up, and looked over to Mal. "Have you been listening to the CB?"

"No, we haven't," Mal said.

"Joe, can I fix you something hot to drink?"

"Oh, man you are a saint, I'd love some coffee if you got any?"

"Me too," Mal said, his eyebrows raised in expectation.

"I'll put on a pot," I said and left them to chat.

Joe winked at Mal. "You better watch it my friend or someone might come along and steal your pretty lady."

Mal smiled and looked at me then headed for the CB's and turned one on. Chaos erupted from it as multiple people were trying to speak at once.

A few snippets came through, "Walmart is totally engulfed," one voice said.

"POP, POP, POP..."

Another cried out, "OH MY GOD, they shot one of the firemen!" I looked on in horror as the reports kept coming.

Turning down the volume he looked to me. "Who is this?"

"We aren't sure, but the mic must be jammed keeping it keyed," Joe said. "Near as we can figure it could be Steve and Pam."

I gasped and dropped one of the mugs on the floor, shattering it in a loud crash. "Pam?" The word squeaked out in pitiful resonance. Shock still gripping my chest I struggled to regain my composure and moved off to find the broom.

Mal came over and took the broom from my shaking hands and began the cleanup while I moved over to the counter for another cup. "They were going into town to grab a few things and called in advising us that Keene was burning. It was right before all of this started broadcasting."

"Are they ok?"

"Not sure but a couple of guys have headed into town to look for them and check on the status of Keene." Joe thanked me for the hot liquid and continued. "We hadn't heard from you since this afternoon and Mike asked me to check on you two. They should be getting to where Steve and Pam checked in soon, but it is anyone's guess. We don't know how bad it is yet, we can only hope they are ok."

"We're fine, if you need to go help in town all is good here," Mal said. "Battening down the hatches after last night."

"Understandable," Joe said, sipping on his coffee. "Unless they call me for some more help, I am just supposed to check on you two."

He finished his coffee and said he wanted to go check on his friend before calling it a night. He donned his gear and headed back out into the snow.

"This is insane," Mal said. He turned the dial on the walkie up again and the chaos continued. More shots were fired and people screaming before a familiar voice came across the walkie. "Steve... C'mon Steve."

We both gasped, they'd found them. "Oh Shit! I hope they're ok," the words came out like it was someone else's voice, they sounded distant, frightened. I couldn't believe this was happening.

The action continued to play out over the walkie. "OK, grab them both. Let's get outta here.

"POP... POP, POP, POP."

More shots, then the radio went dead. Tears welled up in my eyes for fear of our friends. We could hear Meeker and Mal thought he heard Mike, but we weren't sure if the second voice was indeed Mike or someone else.

Mal keyed the mic and called out across the walkie. "This is Mal, anyone got a sitrep on our people?"

A crackle and some background noise came across, then nothing.

Mal repeated the call, "This is Mal, anyone know what's going on in Keene?"

Again, the walkie crackled, and Mike's voice came across in a hurried tone. "Mike here, Steve and Pam are OK. I will be bringing them back to the store, we should probably get together and meet to discuss what's going on in town. Chris is headed to the store to open it now, meet us there in 15, over."

I looked over to Mal in relief, happy our friends were safe. I hurried to get ready to leave for the store. The small country store was the unofficial meeting place where we would visit our friends and talk of various things. Always terrific food, we often found ourselves hanging around chewin' the fat. Now our little store straight outta history was the base of operations to lookout for our local area. Mal opened the truck door, and I hopped in, chattering about Pam and Steve.

"I'm sure they're OK," Mal said.

"I hope so, it is terrifying because it was only yesterday that we were having my head stitched up."

"I know," Mal said. "It is incredible how quick the fall came. In a moment everything descended into chaos."

The look on Mal's face was one of concern. He stared straight ahead as he drove, his mind far away. We were both shocked at the way that things had gone, each in our own thoughts. On numerous occasions we discussed with the others the possibility of civil unrest in this country. I don't think I'd ever considered what that might mean. They were right all along. We should have been better organized.

All we could do now was hope we could somehow manage to pull it all together. Mal steered the truck into the small area behind the store and we headed inside through the back door. Joe, Chris, and Jen had arrived. Fawn stood off in the corner wringing her hands, her eyes red and wide, looking terrified as she waited for Meeker to return.

I joined her and Jen at the small table in the corner, reassuring Fawn that we had heard from Mike and that they were on their way back. Tears flowed down her cheeks as if the faucet had been opened and she dared to hope. Jen handed her a tissue and she gingerly dabbed her eyes, sniffling. We all jumped when the back door flung open, and in walked Meeker and Mike hauling Steve between them. Jen leapt from her chair and ran behind the counter, retrieving the first aid kit while Mal, Joe, and Chris cleared a space at the table they were sitting at for Steve.

Peering around them, looking beyond and out the door my voice became panicked. "Pam? Pam, where's Pam?"

Meeker glanced over his shoulder at me and tipped his head. "She's out in the truck. As soon as Steve is seated, we'll go grab her."

Joe hopped up and hurried to the door. When we got outside and looked in the car, Pam sat stoic, her face was streaked with tears and dirt. She looked over at us. Her voice hitched from the sobbing. "Is Steve alright?"

Joe reached for her, his massive paw of a hand sliding up under her legs, he effortlessly hoisted her from the vehicle. "Not to worry, little lady, I'm sure he's gonna be fine. What do you say we settle you inside and make sure you're OK too, alright?"

She nodded and latched on to his neck, sobbing as he carried her back into the store. Pam was unharmed other than a bump on the head from when they smashed into the telephone pole. Steve was not injured too bad, but it was likely he had a concussion. The two of them were shaken up but other than their truck, we had no casualties.

Pam sniffled and wiped the snot from her nose, trying to sit straighter and control her sobs. "You wouldn't believe it," Pam said.

"What did you see?"

"The whole city of Keene... It's burning!"

"The whole city?"

Pam nodded and continued to cry, trying to wipe the dirt and tears from her face. "I was so scared," she said sniffling. "People were fighting everywhere!"

Keene was a mere twenty minutes away, and although what we saw yesterday was out of hand, we didn't expect this. The room was abuzz with conversation and concerns about what it meant for us. People who lived in the cities were oftentimes vastly different from those of us who lived in the country and it was difficult to understand what was going on. The one thing I did know was that our lives were about to change drastically.

It was only the day after the election, no winner had been declared, and things were out of hand. The groups that went into many cities, whose only purpose was to incite violence, according to what the news reported yesterday. The people were so worked up and volatile that this was quite effective. And it was tearing the country apart.

Once Steve woke up and had his bumps and bruises treated by Mike, we all sat in conversation, each offering their thoughts on where this might lead and what our next steps might be.

"Hey, Steve," I ribbed him. "Do you feel like you have a need to scratch behind your ears?"

Steve looked up confused. "Huh?"

I laughed, "Isn't that what you said to me after our friendly neighborhood veterinarian, Mike, stitched up my head?"

Steve smiled and winked. "Unless I start licking my ass, I'd say he ain't too shabby."

We all laughed. Steve, grabbing hold of his head, chuckled. But Joe was agitated, and Mal asked him what was wrong.

"If those lunatics come out this way, what are we supposed to do? Each of us is an island, in our own space... And I know we each can fend for ourselves but not against mobs of this size."

Chris stood, hands on hips nodding in agreement. "I was thinking the same thing, and they know about the store.... Does anyone remember the people who showed up yesterday at the covered dish?"

Mal sat looking out the front window. "You're right, I remember them. Dani and I left because of the rising tensions. She was stitched up that very afternoon and I was worried if something broke out that her injuries would be compounded."

The others sat nodding and murmuring, Meeker went behind the counter and began fishing around for something. "What are you looking for?" Chris hopped up and joined him behind the counter.

"The local map. I know you have one, I saw it last week."

Chris' eyes lit up with understanding. He hopped up from the table and hurried behind the counter to where Meeker was digging around. Emerging with the map he spread it out on the table for all of us to check out. A star was drawn on the map that represented the store where we currently sat. He brought a pencil and each of us placed an X on the map where our houses were located. Mike, who lived in Keene behind the veterinary clinic, had stayed in the small apartment above the store last night. Mal and I lived north of the store while Meeker, Fawn, and the kids lived down the street, Joe, Steve, and Pam lived the furthest away... and the closest to Keene. Chris and Jen lived above the store with their two boys in the second apartment.

Joe pointed to the map saying, "This is what I mean... We are all over the place and the others? Our friends, our neighbors, people from the range? We're scattered. We need a central location that is out of the way in case anyone is forced from where they live."

"I agree," Mal said. "But where?"

"Here," Meeker said, pointing to the map. "There is an old farm here."

"Where?" Mal asked. "The only thing out there is some woods. I hunt out that way and there isn't even a road, just some snowmobile trails."

"Exactly," Meeker grinned. "An old farmhouse that, believe it or not, is still standing and not in bad shape. When the forest society bought the land fifteen years ago the place was abandoned, but it is still standing, likely thanks to the metal roof. Not that it is wonderful, there has been some vandalism and some windows are broken but we could board or plastic them."

"This is a worthy option," I said. "But how will we find it?"

"How about in the morning we make a quick run to it and check it out?" Mike began packing a few small items in his backpack.

"That sounds like a plan," Chris walked out from behind the counter. "Weather permitting it would be sweet if we could pre-position some things?"

Meeker hopped up from his seat. "Valid thinking. Let's meet up. Here. Early."

"Agreed," Chris stepped in wiping the table.

Mal stood, "Well, it's about that time."

I checked with Pam, making sure she was ok, and we each said our goodbyes and headed for home.

We drove the roads in silence. Each of us with our own thoughts. Once we got home, it was clear someone had been there from the tire tracks in the driveway. Mal looked around the yard but didn't find any footprints, we assumed somebody stopped by, saw that the truck was gone, and decided to come back later. It still made me uneasy after the night before. We still had to contend with the sons of the man we shot, and this weighed heavily on both our minds.

It was getting late, and I was tired. "I say we lock everything down and go to bed. I gotta tell ya Mal, the past two days have worn me right out."

"That sounds like a fabulous idea." He stoked the fire with big chunks of oak for the night.

"I'll fix us a quick snack since we missed dinner."

"Great. You straighten things inside, and I'll finish getting the wood on the fire and fill the wood box."

It didn't take us long to batten things down, chomp on the sandwiches I'd made, and hop into bed. We were both sleeping in a matter of minutes, it had been a long day.

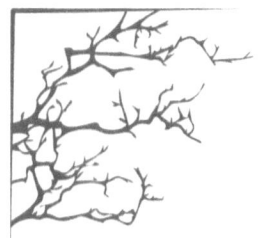

Attack

In the blackness, the sound came from all around. A loud crash shattered my sleep, it sounded like someone was breaking down the side door. Mal jumped from the bed grabbing his .45 and running for the hall. I hunkered down behind the bed once again holding the shotgun. Someone was outside the door and the loud crash echoed through the house again as the axe chopped into the door. A loud crash at the front door sounded like splintering wood, yet another person was chopping through the door.

Mal screamed, "Dani, the front."

I hurried to the living room and took up a position behind the wood box and laid the shotgun loaded with slugs atop the wood aimed at the door.

CRASH!!

The side door cracked followed by the boom of Mal's gunfire.

Pop, pop, pop... silence.

I was terrified for Mal and looked down the hall. I had no cover from that direction and another chop exposed an axe blade through the front door. I fired and the ear shattering sound of the shotgun shook me as the projectile raced toward its target. Clean through the door the bullet raced, a loud cry on the other side told me I'd hit the mark.

The shiny edge of the axe remained in the door, but we heard the sound of a truck pulling out of the driveway in a hurry, raining gravel on the porch.

Mal came from down the hall. "Are you ok?"

"Other than a little ringing in my ears, I'm fine."

"Did you see anyone?"

"No, I shot right through the door," I said pointing to the hole in the door.

He took care when he opened the door and peered through the crack into the night. A large orange handled Fiskars axe hung from the door where they'd tried to smash through it. Mal opened the door a little wider and pulled the axe from it, eyeing it and nodding.

"Nice axe," he grinned. "We'll be keeping this."

"What time is it?"

Mal looked down at his watch. "3:30."

"Might as well put the coffee on. Not likely that I'll be going back to bed."

Mal agreed and tossed some wood into the fire while continuing to pace from door to door checking on each one. He was uncharacteristically unsettled and that alone made me quite uncomfortable. Every sound seemed to echo and each time, I jumped; my anxiety heightening until I yelled at him.

"Would you sit down, dammit?"

He sat in the chair beside the wood stove and looked at me, eyes still darting from one place to another. He reached for the coffee without even a shift in his expression. I handed it to him and stoically, and without a word, took a long sip.

"What is wrong with you?"

"I don't know," he said. "Something is off. Almost like it was too easy to fend them off."

"I get that, I feel it too." My voice faltered trying to sound as though I was not affected, when in reality, he voiced the same grating thoughts I'd had, and it was terrifying because it meant I wasn't just overreacting.

"Why don't you go and get dressed. I'll keep an eye on the doors while you do. Dress for a winter day in the woods, to be on the safe side."

I hurried to the bedroom and pulled out my Under Armour, a pair of jeans, and long sleeve tee shirt. I made sure to put on the warmest socks with my winter hiking boots and grabbed my hoodie before heading back to the living room. Mal did the same while I kept an eye on the doors.

Peering through the crack in the side door I saw movement in the woods behind the shed. A gasp escaped me before Mal reached from behind, covering my mouth. He pointed toward the front and nodded at the location where the shotgun was still sitting behind the wood box. I hurried to the safety of cover and held the gun aimed at the door shaking slightly.

The light was on and would allow for someone to see inside through the hole I'd previously blown in the door. It was glaringly obvious that I was a sitting duck, as if a spotlight were shining on me. In a moment of panic, I broke cover and darted for the small lantern, and as I did a shot came right through the door. A near-miss, as a bullet struck a photo on the wall. It fell, crashing upon the floor, glass shattering.

I screamed and killed the lantern while crawling along the wall near the door. A stream of light shone through the gash in the door where the axe had been, and an eye peered through the bullet hole. Terror racked my body and kept me from moving. I mustered every ounce of willpower and insisted it comply, crawling along the wall all the way around the room, sliding along the baseboard in the dark until I reached where my shotgun lay atop the pile of wood.

Aiming at the hole in the door I'd left earlier, I closed my eyes and pulled the trigger. Half of me hoped I'd miss whoever it was, while the other half wanted death; to kill this asshole once and for all.

Stupidly, closing my eyes caused the shot to go wide, but did take out the light shining through the gash in the door. The man's deep voice cursing from the other side of the door spurred me to action. I racked the weapon and fired again. I had no aim, but continued, ejecting the spent shells and firing again and again, until all five shots had left holes in the once-solid wood door.

Gasping, I leaned back against the wall and drew my Kimber Micro 9 and sat frozen, holding it aimed at the door. A few minutes went by and Mal emerged from the side area and took the gun from my hands.

"They're gone for now," he said. "Come and give me a hand."

I looked up at him, tears welling up in my eyes, "Why?"

He held me close, and I cried into his arms, this was all too much to wrap my mind around. Shock surrounded the past few days, I'd gotten stitches, we'd been attacked twice, and our local city had been burned to the ground. "What is going on?" I cried.

"I don't know," he admitted. "I never would have expected this in only a few days."

He led me to the chair, sat me down, and grabbed the now steaming hot pot of coffee that had been allowed to boil over and headed for the kitchen. Moments later he returned with two cups of coffee and handed me one.

"You might find some grounds in it, but it is decent coffee and hot."

I sipped the warm liquid and my eyes lit up when the smooth taste of chocolate hit my lips. "Mmmmmmm."

He smiled at me and sipped his own before sighing and nodding toward the hallway where the side door stood ajar.

I gasped when I saw it was cracked open. He nodded, "That's what I needed your help with."

Setting my cup on top of the back edge of the wood stove, I hopped up and headed for the door. Mal was right behind me and tried to reach the door before I did. Once I reached it, I understood why. A man lay dead on the stoop, one eye gone. A hole in his eye socket where the bullet entered and a huge mess where it exited. He lay half-on and half-off the stoop, staring upward from his single remaining eye at the clouding sky.

My hands went to my face and Mal slammed the door closed. The place where the doorknob normally sat was nothing more than a hole in the door.

"C'mon we need to barricade this."

"OK, how?"

"Well... I doubt they will break through this," he said pointing to the gun safe.

"Yea but..."

"I have a dolly in the garage." He hopped up and hurried to his coat.

"Oh no...! You're not going out there!" I followed him vehemently objecting to that idea. "They could be out there."

"I have to, we can't defend with the doors wide open."

Tears ran down my cheeks. "Please don't."

"Keep an eye out, OK?"

"I can't... I couldn't bear it if..."

He turned back to me and his eyes softened. "Now how are we going to keep them out with this door broken and you blowing holes in the other one?"

I looked at him sheepishly, eyebrows raised.

"They are gone for now, but we need to hurry before they regain their courage."

"OK," I sniffed and stood taller.

"Ready?"

"Go." I stood outside the doorway with the body of a man at my feet, watching the yard as Mal sprinted for the garage. His headlamp was like a beacon flashing around the barn. "Hurry! Dammit, hurry up...!"

My head jerked from side-to-side, peering into the still-dark morning. It wouldn't be light for hours yet. The tension was like a wrench twisting the muscles in my neck and between my shoulder blades, stretching them like a rubber band drawn too tight, soon to snap.

Mal emerged with a box, dragging the dolly behind him in a sprint for the door. A shot rang out with a loud CLINK striking the dolly and knocking it from his hands. I fired, emptying the magazine into the darkness in the direction of the flash while Mal recovered the dolly and bolted for the door. We slammed it shut and he pulled out a hammer and handful of long nails. Ripping the board from the nearby woodwork he stretched it across the door and began hammering it into place.

"Go!" he shouted. "Load the shotty and grab the other nine mil from the drawer, I can move this with the dolly."

"No, you can't!" I screamed. "Let's do this."

He shoved the dolly under the edge of the massive gun safe and pulled on the dolly. It hardly moved.

"Do it again!"

I put my feet on the wall and my back against the side of the safe and shoved with all I had, and it shifted a few inches toward the door.

"Again," he said.

My legs shook I shoved so hard. Again, it shifted closer to the door.

"One more time."

I yelled through clenched teeth pushing with all my strength as it settled inches from the door. "Again?"

"No, that's close enough, a person could not fit through that small space. I am glad we added the drop boards across all the shutters, the three-quarter plywood should be strong enough... I hope."

"I'm worried, Mal. What do they want?"

"I don't know, babe. Either the guns the others were coming for or payback for killing the fat man."

"What are we gonna do?"

"Right now, I am going to hang some boards across this door. Keep an eye out."

I peered through the holes in the door until he emerged with one of the closet doors to nail over the other door and a board to go across the whole thing. Once he was done, we relaxed. I slumped in the chair rubbing my neck and Mal grabbed the walkie from the kitchen counter, turning it on. He keyed it and called out to the others; it took a few tries before Mike came back across the speaker.

"Go ahead Mal, Mike here."

"Oh man! I am glad to hear your voice," Mal said. "We have been under attack for better than an hour. I think we are hunkered down for the moment, but the location is not safe. I repeat NOT SAFE. We need to relocate to location alpha. Help will be much appreciated come sun-up."

"Roger that. We will assemble the guys and be over shortly. Keep the channel open and listen, we will radio when we are coming in."

"Radio before you arrive, and we will be ready for cover fire if needed."

"Sounds good. Talk soon."

Mal turned to me, stress etching his forehead. "We won't be coming back. At least not for a while. Gather whatever you think we will need. We will likely be the first ones to set up out at the abandoned farm but not the last."

I looked at him horrified. "Leaving?"

"I want to pack up into the living room... everything we can carry, but that we can all load up in a matter of minutes."

Tears welled up in my eyes and I stood looking around the room unsure of where to even begin, or what to pack.

"Dani... Clothes, bedding, cooking, food. Let's go."

"Ok," I whimpered.

"I'm going to grab the guns and put them into the totes as well as the ammo cans."

"Grab the bug out bags, and camping stuff," I called out to him as he started down the stairs to the basement. "Make it quick!" I barked. "I don't wanna be up here all by myself."

He paused two steps down, "I'll be back in a jiffy."

Inside the hour we had gathered everything we thought we could take. He made a list of all the things from the garage that he wanted so that when the others arrived, they could take care of what he wanted. Once all was done, we sat awaiting their call.

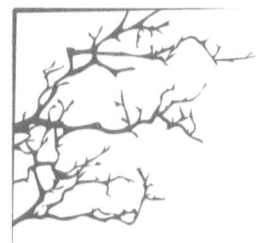

Day Two

The radio crackled to life as the first rays of sunshine crept in through the cracks in the doors and windows. Air rushed past my teeth as though I was releasing a long-held breath. I listened as Mal recounted to the others what had happened and asked that they come help. It was agreed and they would arrive soon. Until then, I busied myself with making one last pot of coffee and something to eat.

The time seemed to crawl by slow and anxiety was crawling up my back like a bug. Twitching and wringing my hands in my lap, I waited for the others to show up. At last, they arrived without incident. The relief was visible across my entire body. Mal pulled the bar from the front door as Joe stepped up on the porch.

"Holy shit, who blew this asshole away?" He said pointing to the guy that lay sprawled across the porch and half onto the snow pile.

Mal opened the door and we saw the man laying in the snow, his skin grey from the cold. His left shoulder was a mass of destruction, with another impact to the side of his neck that exited with a gaping hole.

Mal peeked back into the room at me before shaking Joe's hand, brushing the question off knowing I'd be upset. "I can't tell you how glad we are that you guys are here."

Joe peeked in at me and then grabbed the corpse, dragging it off around the side of the house. He was gone for only a few moments, but I began to pace a nervous circle. "Where did he go?"

"Just around the side of the house, he will be right in, Dani. How about we double check things and make sure we're ready?"

I nodded to him and cast my eyes downward. "I'm sorry, I don't mean to be so jittery, it's that..."

"I know, honey, all of this has been a bit much if you ask me. Things will be better once the others make it here."

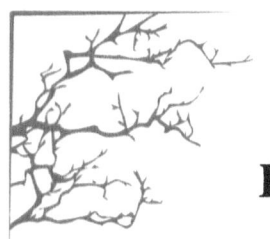

Location Alpha

J oe stepped in followed by most of the other guys who'd pulled into the driveway while he was taking care of the body. Pam was with them bringing some muffins and coffee for the whole gang. In twenty minutes, we were loaded. Mal packed up everything but the kitchen sink, it seemed. The house was locked tight, and the trucks began pulling out of the driveway. Each vehicle took a different route in hopes that if anyone was watching, they would find no clear direction in our movements for the assailants to follow.

We made a lap around the back roads and were the last vehicle to go for the location once we were sure no vehicles were following. Mike stood at the entry to the trail with a snowblower that he used to cover the vehicle tracks into the driveway which wound round a hillside to the run-down house, obscuring it from view of the trail.

Once we arrived the others pitched in and went right to stashing supplies. Meeker had a fire going warming the place up. Yesterday they brought a new stove pipe and wood for the stove. I brought our hammocks and we strung them up in the main room keeping most of the others closed off for the time being. I was quite sure it would not be long before we would see the others as well and planned to prepare the place, ready to house our friends, and perhaps more, in what was sure to be rough times ahead if things had gone so awry so soon.

We sat around and visited for a time before Jen, Pam, and I began organizing one of the smaller rooms off the main living room. We carried in a table and some chairs. An old shelf was found in another room and we tossed it up against the far wall and began to unload some of the supplies that we'd brought.

Chris came in and looked around, "What are you ladies up to?"

"Hey Chris," I greeted, glancing at him for a second before going back to my task. "Setting up the infirmary."

"Well now, Dani, are you and the girls planning to need it?"

Jen glared at him. "You best hope we don't need it. Did anyone forget what happened last night in Keene?"

"Babe... I didn't mean to...."

"I thought not... Now, Christopher, why don't you help out by getting the rest of the supplies in here. We will want to take notes on things that would be a priority if we need to come here."

"Woah..." I snickered and smiled at her. He knew he was in the doghouse. When Jen called him Christopher, he was going to hear about it later, that was for sure.

After he left, she glanced at me and then to Pam and we all giggled. "Sometimes, he needs a kick in the ass."

We laughed again and then hunkered down to establish what supplies we had and make lists of priority items for each of the others. Should they need to go in a hurry, they wanted to make sure to grab first the things highest on the priority list.

For another hour or so, we settled in, had a quick bite to eat, and discussed the day's plans. Meeker and Fawn were going to grab the kids and her mom, who lived with them, and go ahead and relocate this morning. They lived in the trailer park that was a little too close to some of the unsavory types that before now somehow went unseen. Mike was going to remain at the location for the time to keep watch and make sure the tracks stayed covered. Mal and I planned to go check on the old woman.

"I'm worried about her, Mal."

"I know, Dani. We will go straight there, alright?"

"OK, sorry. I don't mean to be so pushy. I have a bad feeling is all."

We each got ready to head out. We'd leave all at once, so Mike could cover the tracks. Meeker would stop for Mike's things that he'd left in the small studio above the store and bring them back to the location with them when they returned, and the others would be discussing the move this afternoon. Chris was afraid to leave the store unattended and wanted to remain, but Jen wanted to go, telling him that she was sure they would be a target, just for being a store. They bickered on the way out the door. I figured we would see them today.

On the drive, I stared at the white branches of the snow-covered trees flying by, wondering if we could somehow persuade our new friend to join us for the time being. She was old and could not possibly fend for herself against these kinds of predators. As the crow flies the old house was through the woods and down the other side of the hill. Not far from where our house was, but the road went all the way out and around the mountain to circle to the top. Just a short drive from where our house was, there was no way she would go unnoticed in that big house atop a hill.

We got closer and as we drove up the road, a stream of black billowing smoke could be seen rising from where our house sat. We paused at the end, near the turn off, and several people were visible through the woods jumping up and down cheering at the blaze that was once our home. Tears welled up in my eyes and Mal shook with anger, all but boiling over. He gripped the wheel and began to turn the truck toward them, but I grabbed it.

"Mal, we can't. Let's go for the old woman."

He jerked his arm away. His eyes blazing as he opened his mouth to speak but I cut him off.

"Please... We can't do anything right now, there's too many of them."

"I'm gonna kill those assholes. I built that house with my own hands."

"I know babe, but we can't take all of them on ourselves."

Mal glared at them and took note of the vehicles that were in the driveway. We continued up the hill. I was sad too. I'd been staying at that damn apartment on the other side of the state for a stupid job and now it is all we have. I tried to be encouraging, but there was nothing that could be said.

We were lucky to get out not only with our lives, but with all the stuff we did take. We cleaned the place out and what we didn't take he placed in the old tree stash that he created last summer. The idea came from a YouTube channel he'd been following. I think he hid more stuff but wasn't sure. I did know that we took most of our things from the house.

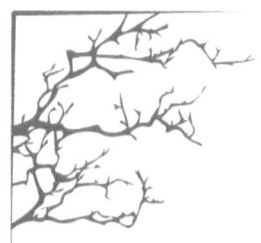

Murderers

We knew something was wrong the minute we reached the top of the hill. Her house too, was now a pile of smoldering rubble. Panicked, I jumped from the truck and ran toward the building. Mal hurried behind me calling out, "Slow down, Dani. We don't know what we're walking into."

I caught sight of him over my shoulder like a flash, but it was long enough to miss seeing the lump in the snow. Face first, I fell, unable to stop myself from tripping and plowing into the snow. I found myself laying face to face with the kind old woman, whose body was sprawled in front of me.

Horrified, I flipped over and crab-crawled backward, slipping in the blood that colored the snow, turning it into a deep crimson slush, that covered my hands and feet.

The scream stunned Mal for a second, my hysteria unchecked as I continued to crawl backwards away from the bloody mass before me.

"Who would do this?" A voice I did not entirely recognize as my own screeched.

"Dani... Dani, calm down."

I heard his voice, but fear and revulsion rocked my senses. The screaming was all I could hear. My own screams echoing through the trees as the sound rolled down the hillside. I'd flipped back to my stomach and was trying to crawl away from the whole scene but Mal grabbed me and held me down. I wanted to escape, but the flight impulse subsided, and I buried my face in his chest and sobbed.

I don't know how long we sat in the snow, but it was too long. A loud rumble had begun traversing the long driveway and Mal sprang into action, hoisting me up and tossing me into the passenger seat. The truck was shifted and locked into four-wheel drive and Mal barreled down the driveway. When the other truck came into view, he pressed the pedal harder, calling for more speed, which it readily provided. I sat in the seat and fumbled for the seat belt when it seemed the other truck would not give on the narrow drive. They swerved, landing in the snowbank, and we rushed on by.

"Mal... We need to go back!"

He glared at me and continued to drive without a word.

"What if they think it was us?"

"They won't," he replied his voice angry. "It was them."

"Them who? Mal, I don't understand."

He turned to me and in essence spat at me. "Them... They're the ones that hurt her and burned our house."

"What?" I turned to him shouting. "How do you know?"

"Dani, didn't you notice the truck? It was the same one that was parked in our driveway."

When we got to the end of the driveway others were waiting. We didn't expect more, and Mal swerved, landing us in the ditch.

"Hurry!"

I scrambled for my purse, but he screamed, "Leave it!"

Each of us had a small everyday pack, our AR-15's, and nothing more. He hunkered down behind the truck and I fell into place next to him, setting the AR up across the bed of the truck unsure of what we were going to do. He shoved the walkie at me and screamed, "Call the others! Tell them where we are and that we will be going across the trails to the location. Make sure they know we might need help."

As I squeezed the button on the walkie a loud barrage of gunfire rang out. I tried to shout over it but was unsure if anyone had heard me. Mal began to take aim on the gang squatted behind the old Toyota Tundra.

Pop... Pop, Pop. He fired and one fell over the side of the hood. More gunfire followed and again Mal peered over the side of the truck and fired a few shots injuring another. His screams felt almost satisfying and I raised myself up and took aim through the window at a scruffy looking guy with an unkempt beard and a ball cap on. Slowly, I squeezed the trigger and the glass shattered. The man slumped before my eyes. A mixture of anger and disgust rose up like bile in the back of my throat.

The truck that we'd run off the driveway was now coming, and we were outnumbered. From the back of the truck a man lobbed a burning Molotov Cocktail our way. It smashed in the back of our truck, sending fiery burning liquid all over both the truck and us. I rolled in the snow while Mal continued to fire at them. He didn't realize it, but his back was on fire. I tossed snow on him and rubbed it down, putting out the blaze. They continued to toss things at us and shoot, but for the most part we had them pinned as much as they had us—until. Something they sent over exploded, ripping through the tailgate of the truck and tossing shrapnel out in all directions.

Mal spun and fell to the ground. The debris shot out into the assailants, stunning them as well. Thick black choking smoke rose from the back of the truck and I grasped desperately at Mal.

"Get up! Mal, get up we gotta go."

Mal gasped and struggled for his feet. Tucked up under his arm I grasped the two packs and helped him limp into the thick woods. Beyond the steep drop ahead, a Dollar General was only recently opened. We slid down the hillside and Mal crumpled.

"Go, Dani. Find the others."

"Not without you!"

I looked around for something to help me get him to the house that was down the mountain from here. All we had to do was make it across the road and then we would be on the snowmobile trails and perhaps help would be waiting... I hoped.

I hurried to the front of the store, but remembered I'd left my purse in the truck. I had no money.

"Screw it."

Without even bothering to look around, I snatched up one of the long red toboggan sleds and hurried back to Mal. He struggled and fought me to go, making it even more difficult to drag him onto the sled.

I shoved him hard, rolling him onto his back, three-fourths of the way onto the sled. "Shut up Mal. Now get on the damn sled."

He groaned and shimmied himself the rest of the way. I grabbed the packs and tossed them on top of him, handing him one of the AR-15's in hopes he could fire it. Slinging the rope across my middle, I grasped it and pulled as hard as I could. To my surprise, it slid on the ice easily, but the snow on the other side of the road was deeper than I'd thought. Looking back at him, the color in his face grew pale and fear overwhelmed me, but I kept pulling.

The snow was deeper in the thick of the trees, but I couldn't stay on the trail. First, it was too obvious, with nowhere to hide, but it also went in the wrong direction. My boots sank through the snow and the sled dug in with the weight of Mal onboard. The going was slow, and I was getting tired but giving up was not an option.

I'd been going nonstop, head down, and paused to rest a moment. Something was off. I looked around the stand of trees and couldn't tell which way the road was. Coming down that hill I should have hit a road by now. It was the road that would take me to the trail where the abandoned house was.

"Shit!"

My head jerking in all directions in a near panic I was becoming overwhelmed. Tears ran down my frozen cheeks while disbelief and agonizing fears emerged immobilizing me.

"Don't worry Mal, I'll find them," I said looking to him lying on the sled. He'd passed out some time back which worried me but also quieted our escape. The bumps were hard on him.

SNAP!

"Shit, what was that?"

I froze. Someone was out here with us. We'd left a trail a blind man could follow between the sled marks and the blood. Second guessing myself I now questioned if I should have stayed on the snowmobile trail.

Anxiety gripped me, a nagging in the back of my mind, telling me that I'd made the wrong choice. Not only was the snow deep and every step a struggle, slowing me down, but now the trail was unmistakable and even easier to follow.

"Dammit, I need to get us outta here," I whispered to myself while looking everywhere at once.

The bullet passed close enough to move my hair and I fell flat to the ground, my heart racing so fast, it was the only sound I could hear. It beat so loud I swore someone could hear it through the trees.

"OK, stand up," I told myself. "I've had it with these assholes."

Growling, I began to visually search for the assailants. There... I'd spotted them. Not only that... I recognized them.

"These freaking people never quit," I cursed, sneaking to another tree for a better look.

They stood around like stooges fighting with Mal's favorite AR-15. I giggled a little because I knew they'd never figure out the little quirks in this baby. Full on running for the cover of a massive bull pine, I slammed into the tree and fell to the ground. Both of them stood staring at me like I was crazy, while they continued furiously banging on the gun.

I lined him up in my sights and squeezed the trigger, not once but three times.

POP, POP, POP...

He crumbled to the ground in a heap.

She reached for the gun and aimed it at me as I stormed toward her holding my Kimber out in front of me, stomping through the snow, anger fueling my advance without thought. She held the gun up and pulled the trigger. Nothing happened.

I snatched it from her hands and slammed her in the left side of her head above the eyebrow with the butt of the gun. She fell to the ground, grasping at the wound and crying out.

"Please, don't kill me."

"This is his favorite," I scowled. Then raised it, ejected the spent round, and chambered another, all the while glaring at her. Flicking the safety on, I flung it over my shoulder and kicked snow at her before turning away. In the struggle I noted the smoke that rose into the air representing where our house was. I now knew where I was, and where the trail would pick up that went by the old, abandoned house.

Suddenly jerked backward, I was thrown off balance. She'd grabbed the rifle from my shoulder. She pointed it in my face. "Malachi's stupid little princess," she sneered and pulled at the trigger. Again, nothing.

Now I was pissed off, I pulled my gun from its holster, pointed it at her and squinted. Her eyes widened as the recognition hit her.

Through gritted teeth I growled, "Here's your tip, bitch!"

My eye twitched and I squeezed the trigger. The shot rang out and she fell to the ground, the single round obliterating her eye socket and knocking her head backward. She sank to her knees and flopped over onto her side.

Snatching up the gun and racing to Mal, I grabbed the rope to the sled and made my way to the trail. I had to find help before any of the others found me. He needed to be carried or our trail would give away the location. A plan began to hatch inside my head as I trotted down the trail, now much easier to pull the sled, being on the hard packed snow.

A little way before the turn off to the secondary trail I tucked him under the low hanging limbs of a pine tree. It offered a hidden space for him, but also some shelter from the elements.

Not pulling the sled made me feel like I had wings as I jogged down the smaller trail that led to the house to find help. The driveway had been snow blown over once again, so I trekked through the trees around to the side of the house. Rapping on the window for warning, I hurried to the side door and flung it open.

"I need help." The words came out in giant gasps.

Mike scrambled to his feet. He and Joe followed me out the door in seconds and we were trotting to the pine tree for Mal.

"He's not far," I panted.

Mike ran up to me. "What happened?"

"I'll fill you in when we get back, but he's been shot. Didn't you hear my call for help on the walkie?"

"No. We didn't hear anything from anyone."

In a flash the men snatched up the sled on either side and hurried up the trail carrying his limp body. Tears ran down my cheeks as I trailed behind them praying, hoping we were not too late.

All the members of our small group had chosen to make the transition for the time being to the old farmhouse and had made it to the location. The house which had seemed ample to begin with felt small now. I was relieved to find that all of our friends were at the place, but I couldn't settle down. Mal was in with Mike, who wouldn't let me in the room we'd set up as the infirmary. Pam assisted him and promised to take care of him, but it didn't help my nerves much. The door opened and Mike emerged, wiping his hands. Blood was smeared across the front of his shirt and the room began to spin, I felt faint. Darkness circled in on my vision and everything went black.

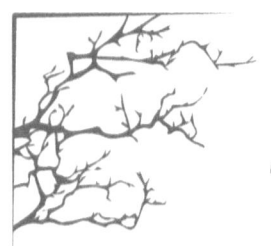

Touch And Go

The bright light pierced my eyes. Fluttering eyelids beckoned me to consciousness, and I tried to sit up. Fawn's firm grip held me down. "Easy does it."

"Wha? What happened?" Confusion clouded my senses.

"Well..." Mike said, standing with his hands on his hips.

"Did you forget to tell us about the shard of metal you managed to pick up?"

"I don't..." I offered and looked around the room. "Metal?"

"Yeah," Jen said holding up a shard of jagged metal about the size of a silver dollar. "Like this?"

"What is that?"

"That, was embedded in your back," Mike said.

I looked around the room confused, blinking at the others, still unsure of what had happened. All at once tears flowed, streaming down the sides of my face and into my ears. I was filled with panic and sorrow, along with gratitude, making for an emotional moment. I had no idea that I'd been hit with a piece of the exploding truck.

"I thought the blood on me belonged to the old woman."

"Old woman?"

"Jen, they... they..." The sobbing grew, with thoughts of the old woman laying in the yard, half dressed, blood-covered snow surrounding her.

"It's ok, shh, we can talk about all of this later."

"Oh my God!" Panic gripped me harder. "Mike... Mal? Where's Malachi?"

"He lost a sizable amount of blood." His expression changed to concern. The worry was in his eyes and it wasn't positive.

"Can I see him?"

"I will let you, but Dani... Let him rest."

I nodded and Joe lifted me from the bed, helping me balance. The room spun again when I stood up and I had to pause and wait for the dizziness to subside. A gasp escaped involuntarily when I looked at him, the peaceful look on his face coupled with the pale color of his skin. I kissed his forehead and whispered in his ear.

"Please be ok, Mal."

Joe steadied me as we walked out to the living area and Fawn brought over a cup of hot tea. The warm liquid soothed my anxiousness with its sweet herbal aroma. I could taste the lavender along with some chamomile, lightly sweetened with the unmistakable flavor of honey. A few sips in and I was ready to recount what had happened.

I explained how we'd promised to put more wood in the shed for the old woman. Everyone gasped when through tears I offered vivid details of our house engulfed in flames. The shudder was visible, and Jen turned away when I explained the blood on my clothes and how we found her in the snow and what happened after. I guessed I got hit with some of the shrapnel from the explosion I postulated.

Mike sat nodding. "That makes sense,"

Fawn placed her hand on my shoulder. "But Dani, didn't you feel it?"

"I had a pain, but I thought it was from pulling Mal."

After I explained about the two attackers, anger welled up within me. Those two plagued us from minute one. Something in the way that the waitress acted the day before the election didn't sit right. Now that I'd had time to think about it, it was something in the way she'd glared at us from the waitress station.

My head snapped to the side. "Chris, I think we were targeted, and your store as well."

"What? Why?"

"It was an odd mannerism at the diner. I recall being annoyed at the way she hung all over Mal, but now I am not so sure it was simply a little flirting. In the woods... she knew Malachi's name. We'd never seen her before the diner, but then again at the polls, and once more at the grocery store in town. I am sure it was the tubby guy with her who hit me in the head."

The excitement was making my head hurt and the stitches on my back pulsed with fire when I tried to move. I think better if I pace but right now pacing was out of the question.

After a few more sips of tea, I continued. "At the old woman's house, they were with the bunch that came and blew up Mal's truck. We'd never seen the others before, but of all the houses to burn down why ours? We were attacked when they were lookin' for guns... and I recall the guy saying we belonged to the gun club."

"But Dani, why do you think they were targeting me?"

"That night after the election in the barn. We left early because Mal was sensing some bad vibes from those guys."

I cast a quick glance over my shoulder. "Mike, you remember them, right?"

"As a matter of fact, they were trying hard to start some shit."

"I don't know if they followed us or if they knew you were having chats in your store. New people came to the potluck, that family that moved into... Dammit what farm was that?"

"Jen you were there. Remember the woman that I kidded with for saying *y'all*?"

"Oh, yes... The Robert's farm."

I knew I was reaching, but something was off. I needed the others to help piece it together. The town burned down, our house, the old lady. These people were here for no other reason than to bring this chaos. I was sure of it... I needed them to know it too.

"Yes, that's it."

"What is?"

"The farm, her husband or whatever was very gruff, kept glaring at those guys. Something was off with the whole thing. Do you think they were looking for the guns?"

Joe stood with his hand on his chin pondering the pieces of the puzzle. I couldn't tell if I was on to something or my brains were scrambled from the past few days.

Mal moaned from the other room and Mike hopped up and made for the door, waving for the rest of us to stay put. My hands shook with anxiety as I waited for him to return with an update on his condition. A few moments later he emerged and the look on his face was troubling. One of worry and concern. I began to cry, and Pam scooted up next to me, hugging me to her and glaring at Mike.

"He's ok, Dani." Mike patted me on the shoulder, reassuring me.

I looked up at him, tears filled my eyes. "Then what's wrong?"

"I was troubled, thinking about how we could find more supplies if he needed it. He lost a lot of blood and I am concerned about that. He is not out of the woods yet, but it is not critical."

He stood wiping his brow and fidgeting with the rag. "Do you happen to know his blood type?"

"O-positive, I think."

Mike looked around the room. "Anyone else have type-O blood?"

Meeker, Fawn, and Joe were all O-positive with Steve type A. Chris was O-negative. Mike nodded with a pleased look on his face. "Does anyone have any issues that would keep them from donating some if need be?"

Meeker stepped forward looking down. "I doubt he could handle all the badassery that goes along with my extremely potent blood."

Fawn smacked him, "Are you kidding me?"

The levity was exactly what the room needed and Meeker volunteered to be the first to donate if needed.

"I've never done a person-to-person transfusion, but it is possible. Let's make sure to keep Meeker hydrated. We'll start with him if we find we need to."

I couldn't help the tears that began to well up again, all of this was too much. I was exhausted, overwhelmed, and the pain in my back and head had begun to throb and pulse. Pam, her eyes soft and gentle, offered me some more tea and a bit to eat. I'd not eaten since breakfast and it was late afternoon. I leaned back sipping the hot lavender and chamomile tea, nibbling on a PB&J. The sweet flavor of the peanut butter and jelly made things feel brighter for some reason. It wasn't long before the exhaustion took over and I nodded off, fretful worries for Mal in the forefront of my mind.

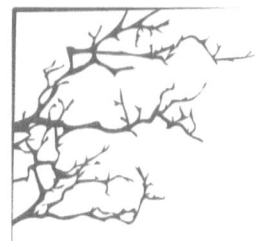

News

A loud noise startled me awake and the pain shot down my spine when I sat straight up in search of where it was coming from. Steve and Meeker were covered in snow and shaking it off when I cried out.

Once the world quit spinning, I asked. "Is everything alright?"

Meeker glanced over to me and offered a lopsided smile that almost looked painful. "We went by your house."

"And?"

"Well, the house is gone, burned right to the ground."

My head hung but I had no tears left to cry. "I figured," I said dejected.

"But..." he countered. "The barn is fine, there was nothing inside they felt they wanted I guess."

"Idiots," I whispered under my breath.

"Best part is the cache is untouched, buried by snow and the wood he'd stacked on top of it."

"Cache?" I looked up at him stunned. He'd said nothing about a cache. "What cache?"

"We all did it right before the election," Meeker said, looking sheepish because it was obvious that Fawn had no idea and was glaring at him.

"C'mon ladies," Steve choked. "How are we supposed to impress you by saving the day if you know all of our secrets?"

Pam glared at him, while Jen looked at Chris in an accusing way. "When did you plan to tell us about this?"

Joe stepped in to save the guys. "We started talking about the volatility a couple of months back during the campaigning when it was clear storm clouds were growing per se. Issues hanging on the horizon like an ominous warning. It was part of the plans that included getting Mike here," he said pointing to Mike. "As well as having all the extras on hand. We took some of them and stashed them in case we needed them."

"I knew Mal had put some things we didn't take into that small space he'd camouflaged. Is that the cache, Joe?"

"It is one, Dani. But we each made much larger ones before then. Mal was the one who got us thinking about it."

Meeker glanced at Steve with a knowing look and then to Chris and Jen. There was more. I had a feeling this was not going to make any of us happy. "There's more, isn't there?"

Meeker looked at Steve again, who began to speak. "Chris, the store is gone, as are a few other buildings in the center of town. We spoke to Robin, who told us what happened."

"Who's Robin?" Pam and I blurted out in unison.

"Her and her husband are the ones that bought the Robert's farm. They were helping a couple of the other families that had been burned out."

"Is everyone alright?" Jen's hands went to her throat gasping.

"They seem to be," Steve said. "Chris," he paused looking over at him. "They found your cache and tossed it all over. It was as if they were looking for something specific."

Chris grinned, "I bet they were."

I was confused and looked from him to the others. "I don't understand. How can you sit there grinning?"

"What I left in the cache was nothing more than extras, like the one Mal left. Anything real and all of the guns and ammo are here and in a secondary place. Being in town and the local store, I didn't feel comfortable having it all in one place, or even nearby."

Steve stood by nodding the corner of his mouth raising. "Damn. You're good."

He and Meeker shared a look. "So, Chris," Meeker said. "I hope you don't mind but we gave the stuff that was there to the families that were in town. We were a little worried about how you'd feel about it, but both of us are willing to share what we have stashed. They were so devastated, we had to help."

"The buildings are insured if things ever go back to normal. And we have more than Jen, the kids, and I need. I'd have done the same." He reached out for Steve's shoulder and nodded to Meeker. "Besides, I've been doing this kind of thing for years. I have squirreled away more than this."

Jen looked at him, her mouth opened in a gasp. "You have?"

"Honey, I ordered things in bulk for the store. Mal and Joe over here went in on some of it also."

Fawn stood up. "Meeker, you have some explaining to do." She smiled a crooked smile and kissed him on the cheek then gathered the kids and sat them at the table for dinner. "Jen, call the boys. Let's eat before it gets cold. We can talk more about things while we eat." She looked at Steve and Meeker dripping in the entry, "You two get out of the wet clothes and quit dripping all over the floor."

The meal was hearty, with a solid beef stew and biscuits. I ate hungrily and listened as the rest began to talk of months back when they hatched the plan to squirrel away a few items. I knew Mal was into this prepping thing and he and the guys would practice things other than shooting on range days but was clueless about how much he did. A small cloud of sadness rolled over me and I began to wonder if he didn't tell me because he didn't trust me or if he thought I would say something about it, or think he was stupid.

The rest of the news was worse. The riots had burned the whole of Keene to the ground. Almost nothing remained and many were dead. The cities were worse, and the national guard was called into these to control the outright war zones they'd become. The current President declared Martial Law and the government was fractured at the very core. Some politicians called it a move to steal the election, while others hailed him a hero in the never-ending battle for power. DC was burning and Marines surrounded the White House protecting the President. No winner in the election could be determined and fraud was rampant.

As I listened to them recount what they'd heard, my mind wandered and I inadvertently blurted out, "A modern day Rome."

Pam walked over. "What was that Dani?"

"All of it similar to Rome," I looked up. "Destroyed by its own arrogance."

The room fell silent, and we ate, filled with thoughts of what might come next. None of us thought our country's demise would be so steep, nor so quick. Questions rose in my mind and fear for what came next clouded my thoughts.

The room was so silent, a crash from the other room made everyone jump.

"Mal?" I cried out.

Mike was sprinting for the room when the door opened a crack. Mike arrived with Joe hot on his heels in time to catch Mal before he fell to the floor.

"Why didn't someone wake me for some of that awesome smelling stew?" He slumped into their grasp.

Mike led him away. "Oh, no you don't. Back to bed with you."

"But..." he said weakly.

"No but's. You're not strong enough to be up and around."

"Can I sit with him?"

"Of course, Dani. Perhaps you can give him a bit of broth too," Mike smiled.

Chris grabbed my arm and held me back as the other two put him back to bed. I glared at him and shook off his grip.

"I'm sorry, Dani, I didn't mean to startle you. It's just..."

"What?" I snapped.

"Dani," Pam stepped up. "We don't think you should tell him what is going on quite yet, is all." She shot Chris a look and he slumped away. "Men, they're always so abrupt. He wanted to catch you before you went to Mal. With him being so weak, we are worried. Before you go in check with Mike first, ok?"

"Ok." I looked to Chris and shot him a smile and a quick nod. He half smiled back and gingerly sat down in the chair with Jen scolding him for being so gruff.

We agreed to keep the happenings to ourselves for now and wait for morning to see what it all looked like. I knew Mal would ask, but I resolved to tell him nothing new.

I sat with him, offering sips of warm tea and water, feeding him broth from the stew. He complained a little, teasing me. "Hey, why do you get all the meat and taters and all I get is the juice?"

I grinned at him, chomping on a whale of a piece of stew meat, "Doctor's orders."

He scowled but raised an eyebrow and winked in my direction. "I won't tell if you won't."

He was beginning to come back to being himself. I let out a long sigh and gave in, offering him small bites. Relieved that some of the humor was there, a smile emerged. It wouldn't last long once he found out about what was happening. He wouldn't be up and around for a while but, he would want to know what was going on.

We will tell him tomorrow. Tonight... I'm happy he is alive.

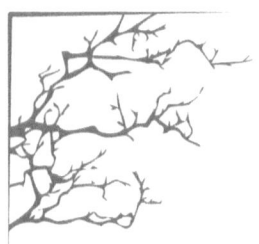

Day Three

J en called out from the other room, waking Mal. He tried to sit wincing in pain. "What's going on?"

"I'm not sure. I'll go check."

A gentle brush against my hand as I turned to leave made me pause and look back at him. He smiled at me. Tilting my head, I lingered a moment. His color looked better today. I looked at him pursing my lips, then the corners of my mouth turned upward. I smiled back and squeezed his hand.

"I'll be right back."

In the kitchen Jen was staring at her phone. She had a signal. We all rushed to check out the small device where videos played showing chaos in the major cities. The small news feed flipped from one location to another with buildings on fire and angry people screaming in the background.

I gasped at the sight of it and my head jerked around to Steve. "Was this what Keene looked like?"

"No Dani. Not even close. In Keene it was small groups of people, like the ones we saw at the barn. This? This is something else."

"I don't think what happened in Keene was a bunch of ticked off citizens. I think that was staged. We've been seeing this all summer with riots in various places and it always appeared to be contrived. This is more like the masses have had it with politics. Look at them," he said pointing to the small screen.

We all sat wide eyed, aghast, taking in the images in the video. The stream cut out, replaced with a black screen and warning. *The content in this video violates platform standards.*

"Wait, What?" Chris yelled. "Now facts go against the rules? What the hell is going on?"

I shrugged; this was nothing new. "C'mon Chris, censorship has been alive and well in this country for years. This is the reason for all of this. The art of misinformation. People intentionally cause confusion so that no one is paying attention to what is going on in back room deals." I turned and walked away. I'd seen enough to know that there was nothing to see. What I could see was our home burned, an old lady dead, and Mal shot. That was what I saw.

I was always so fearful and Mal took care of me. And now he lay shot, the country in chaos, and us on the wrong side of the line. Never once did it occur to any of us that where we lived in relation to the issues would matter so much. At the door to the room, I paused and looked back at them. They all stood around the table trying to get the small screen to play something.

"You know..." Everyone looked at me. "This might be the beginning and we are like those who witnessed the start of the Revolutionary War."

All of a sudden, the world was twisted and out of focus. All that we thought, believed, and held as truth... was shaken to the core.

"Hey Dani, I think you might be confused, don't you mean Civil War?" Steve called out after me.

"No... I know the difference. We may be fighting each other, but make no mistake, our war is against the destruction of the country. We are defending the very Constitution of this country. Fighting for freedom against tyranny that would destroy the rights our forefathers fought to secure. Now we fight to keep them."

The room was silent, and all stared at me. Having never attended their meetings, I rarely weighed in on matters. I may have seemed aloof, but I was very sure on where I stood... and Mal knew that too.

A tear rolled down my cheek, "In case anyone needs a history lesson," I began. "We are not a democracy..."

Meeker's eyes widened, and his mouth opened to speak.

Before he could, I continued on my tirade. "We are a Republic. The similarities end with the basic structure of elected officials and the ability to vote. A democracy is essentially mob rule. It operates on the premise of majority rule and no constraint on the government. Most have no idea because it has been called a democracy for so long, indoctrinating us since the 1930's. But this is not what our forefathers created. That's not all, they deliberately created it this way to avoid this very thing. A Republic does not go by mob rule tactics where the brainwashed will vote for their own demise. It set up the Constitution to regulate the decisions, to ensure the rights of the people would remain. In this structure, the government is constrained, and each individual has sovereignty over themselves. Painting this country as a democracy is how these overreaching laws have been created."

I gasped for a breath while the others stood staring at me like a bugle sounded across the land. "Our country is broken. It has been fractured before our very eyes." I said and hung my head. Casting my eyes upward. "And we... are behind enemy lines."

"Dani, what do you mean?" Joe's eyebrows raised up, with a deep crease in the center.

"We need to leave here. Make no mistake, this country will snap. Many may be brainwashed into thinking this mob rule mentality works but they will find out when something, a right they themselves care about, is stripped away. Then they will cry out, but it will be too late."

Murmuring began amongst them, nodding and realization of what had struck me so hard, as it began to become clear to them.

"I fear we are no longer indivisible. And the fracture is to come, drawing lines and borders."

Jen turned off the small device and stood up from the table. "I'll get some breakfast on. Coffee anyone?"

Chris grunted at her and the rest of us nodded and the mood in the room had shifted to one of pensive reflection on all that I'd said. I opened the door and went in to check on Mal who was sitting up on the edge of the bed looking at me with a crooked smile.

"Babe, you shouldn't be up."

"Aww lemmy be, I can't lay in here while everyone else gets the fun of listening to you spout history."

I glanced at him, sheepish, "You heard that?"

He laughed and winced. "I can as easily rest on the sofa, can't I? I'm tired of being segregated."

I smiled at him, "Now who could resist that little beggar boy look. I'll go find Mike."

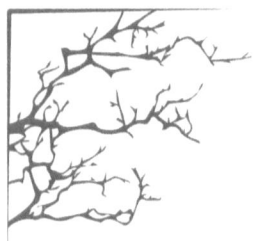

Recon

Mike and Joe moved Mal to the sofa, and breakfast was spent talking about the past few days, as well as the next ones. After all, we couldn't sit out here in the woods, supplies would last a while, but not that long. I'd planted a thought and question in everyone's mind about what this was.

Joe's voice raised, "Listen Meeker, we need some intel, we have no idea what is going on out there."

All while Mike and Chris were going back and forth on the outcomes, speculating on the lack of real news and what we needed to do. The noise level in the room was growing until... Pam shrieked.

"Someone is outside!"

Steve hopped up and ran to his wife, quieting her. Joe and Meeker made for the side door while me and Chris each took a window that hadn't been boarded up. The boards reduced our visibility and Mal was cursing that we hadn't set up a watch yet.

Joe and Meeker slipped out the door and Fawn began to cry, fearful that Meeker would be hurt. Jen hurried to her, hunkering them both in the tall-backed chair that sat in the far corner. She cooed at her to keep her quiet. Mike brought Mal his gun and kneeled on the floor with the AR-15 stretched out across Mal propped up on the back of the sofa.

The silence, but for the quiet whimpering from Fawn, was agonizing. I glanced at Chris and whispered, "Do you see anything?"

He shook his head no and tipped his head upward in response. I shook my head in a firm no and turned back to the window. Squinting against the rising sun reflecting off the pure white snow, the brightness was blinding. In a flash I caught a glimpse of something. I waved to

Chris and signaled for him to look in the direction I'd seen the movement by pointing with my index and middle fingers to my own eyes and then out the window toward the movement. Chris understood in a moment and peered through his window. His view was better without the window reflection, it was shaded by a large pine next to the house and provided him a glare-free view.

There! I'd seen it again. I looked to Chris and he'd seen it too. I crawled over to his position. "Listen Dani, hurry over to the girls and help Mike. We need them to move Mal into the kitchen between the old fireplace stack and the wood stove."

I nodded and crawled over to them. "And Dani? Make sure they all have plenty of ammo, get Jen to help and be quick. I don't think we have much time."

I recounted what needed to be done and helped Mike put the high-backed chair against the wall across from the stove with a clean line of sight to the door. We helped Mal to the chair and I grabbed his ammo can with loaded mags for the AR, his .45 Kimber, and extra ammo. We moved Pam, Jen, Fawn, and the kids to the space between the old chimney and the wood stove, and Mike took over my spot at the second window. I faced the back door which was boarded over and barricaded but indeed an entry point, given enough force.

We knew better than to shoot at anything with Meeker and Joe out in the line of fire and sat rigid, waiting for something, anything, to happen. After a few tense moments, something at the door sent every eye in that direction.

RAP... RAP, RAP.

The distinctive one knock followed by two quick ones.

It was them, the tension rolled off my shoulders releasing my neck from its grip. The door gingerly opened and Meeker came in, followed by Joe and three others. Two men and a young girl.

Meeker waved us to put the guns down and relax. "All is well," he motioned. But, his stance and glances at each of us told another story. "Once we saw it was these two dufuses, we reconned the area and tossed some branches over the breaks in the snow where they'd come up beside the driveway. I think we're good." His eyes flashed and Mal patted my leg.

I glanced down at him and he offered a strained smile. I didn't know who the men were, but the young girl looked to be about twelve and terrified.

Mal did recognize them, holding out a hand to shake. "I'd get up, but Dani would probably hurt me worse than the assholes we ran into."

The men chuckled but it was not in a sincere way. I could not tell if they were trying to laugh off the uneasy joke or if it was something else. It made the hairs on the back of my neck stand up. Something was not right, and I could see Mike thought so too. I glanced at Mal on my way by him to the window where Mike still sat perched and played up to the moment.

"Hey Mike, I'm afraid that moving Mal around so much may have hurt him. I glanced back to Mal who offered an almost imperceptible nod; I am not sure what to give him, can you help me?"

"Sure." Mike rose and headed for our little infirmary with me hot on his heels. I called out over my shoulder, "Pam... These guys look cold and wet, how about some coffee and a hot chocolate for the little lady." Then I looked at Mal, "Grabbing you a little something babe, be right back."

"Thank you, Dani," he winced. "I am a little battered right now."

As soon as I entered the room, Mike grabbed me an pulled me behind the door. "Something is off."

"I agree Mike, but I don't know what?"

"Me either, but how did they know we were here?"

"That's what got me, but there is something more. Something in that laugh at Mal's joke."

"I caught that too," he said shuffling things around on the shelf.

He called out a little louder than normal voice, "Dani can you grab that tin from the table in the corner? I should check his stitches."

I caught on and responded in kind. "Sure thing," and began rattling things around inside the small room.

He glanced over his shoulder before speaking again. "Something is very wrong with the little girl."

"It's in her eyes," I said nodding.

A shuffling sound from behind startled both of us. It was the guy that had laughed. "Hey doc, I heard you say stitches. Can you have a look at my leg?"

Mike turned around. "Sure thing. Let's have a look."

He led him to the table and instructed him to hop up on it. The man did, pulling up his pant leg exposing a long slash in his calf.

"Damn...That must be killing you. What the hell happened?"

"Oh... an accident," the man hissed when Mike touched it with a gloved finger.

"Need some help, Mike? I can assist." He knew better than that, I cringed at the sight of blood.

The man looked at me side-eyed, "You should take that stuff to Mal, I'm sure we can handle it. Right, doc?"

"Sure, sure. No problem." Without looking up from his preparations he waved me off. "I can handle this, Dani, it's only a few stitches. It looks worse than it is."

Mike moved toward the man with a needle, "This is a local. I'm afraid we don't have much of it so you may still feel some of the stitches, but this will help dull it."

The man grunted and Mike stuck the needle in giving him the shot of his life. Within thirty seconds the man slumped to the table.

I was shocked at how fast he was unconscious. "What the hell did you give him?"

He held up the needle and smiled, "Propofol."

"What's that?"

"It is what is used to knock a person out before surgery."

"What now, Mike?"

"You go out to Mal and give him the Advil. That won't mess with his awareness and the other guy will think we are doing stitches. I need to take care of this one."

"Isn't he knocked out?" I looked down counting out four Advil into the palm of my hand.

"It works fast," Mike shot a glance around the room for something to secure him with. "But... it doesn't last that long. I'm going to tie him up and give him something a little stronger until we can figure out what is going on here. There is something not right with these two, but we don't want to jump to any conclusions. They could simply be nervous because of events. No need to overreact, but better safe than sorry. I'll get this stitched up and secure him."

"Ok." I turned and headed for the door with the pills in my hand.

"Dani..."

I stopped at the door and turned back to him.

"Get that little girl away from him."

"Gotcha," I bounded out to the room, closing the door, like nothing at all was amiss.

As soon as I emerged the other guy looked past me for his buddy. "Where is Greg?"

"Who?"

"The guy that went in there with you? And the other guy, where are they?" The threatening tone sent a shiver down my spine. *Keep it together Dani.* I shook it off and continued toward Mal as if it were just another day.

"Oh, him. He's getting that nasty gash on his leg sewn up. They should be out in a couple of minutes."

Handing Mal the Advil and a glass of water, I looked him dead in the eyes and without moving my head shot a glance toward the door

where Mike had the man drugged. A raise of my eyebrows told Mal...
Now there's one.

"Hey Nick, what brings you two out this way?" Mal motioned to
him, his eyes dark and foreboding. Never taking his eyes off him while
lifting the cup to his mouth.

The man never holstered his gun. It was still in his right hand while
the left held the young girl's shoulder. The stance was awkward, if not
rigid, and he looked as though he were ready to bolt through the door
at any second.

I reached for the girl's hand. "Oh my, you look frozen." Looking
into her red face and rubbing her hand between my own. "Let's get you
over to the fire to warm up."

The man's grip on her shoulder tensed, but when I looked at him it
relaxed. "And how about you? A cup of something hot and some food
might warm you two up." I dragged the young girl to the far side of the
stove and wrapped a blanket over her shoulders.

Jen handed her a warm cup of hot chocolate, whispering in her ear
while she leaned over her to grab the coffee pot. "Don't answer, nod.
Are you OK?"

Tears welled up in the young girl's eyes and she shook her head
from side to side. Jen laid a hand on her on the shoulder, "Here honey,
have a seat next to the other kids and stay warm, breakfast will be ready
in a few minutes."

Jen flashed a look at Mal and then to me. Meeker was with Chris
and Joe, hauling in wood, or so it seemed. What they were doing,
was checking the perimeter for any others. Right then they came in,
stomping their feet to knock off the snow. Each with an armload of
wood they tossed haphazard into the wood box. It startled the man,
who spun around raising his gun to them.

"Woah! Woah, guy!" Meeker put his hands up to him. "A bit jumpy
aren't ya?"

"Uh... Sorry, yea there have been some issues."

"Oh, I bet." Meeker brushed past him patting him on the shoulder. "We're all friends here. You can relax." Snatching up a biscuit and getting his hand smacked he giggled and walked past him flopping on the sofa. "C'mon woman, a man could starve round here."

He motioned to the man to have a seat and chomped on his stolen morsel. "So, Nick, what's happening out there? We haven't had any news in about thirty-six hours."

His voice shook and he glanced around the room to discover that Steve was standing behind him. His hand fidgeted on the gun in his lap. Pam walked over smiling at him and handed him a coffee and biscuit to match Meeker's and now his hands were occupied away from his gun and Meeker leaned in toward him. "Your two buddies in the woods? They won't be coming."

He dropped the coffee and biscuit, reaching for his gun. He hadn't noticed Chris come up behind him who jabbed the back of his head. With the barrel of Steve's AR in his side. Chris snarled at him, "I wouldn't."

The man's face went ashen, and he called out, "Greg! Greg, hurry."

Mike smiled from the doorway with a syringe in his hand. "He got a bit sleepy and decided to take a nap."

His eyes shifted to the little girl, "You told them!" Spittle flying from his lips as he lurched toward her and the other children. "I warned you what would happen."

Joe slammed a log across his head and the man crumpled to the floor. A trickle of blood oozed from the gash left behind. Mike checked him, "He's still breathing, bring him in here with his buddy."

Once the two were subdued, the little girl began to sob. Pam put her arm around her cooing, "You're safe now. What's your name?"

She sniffled and wiped her nose. "Susan." Her voice hitching, she gulped for air. "They..." Her words trailed off.

"Did they hurt you?" Mal spat, rage welling up within him and trying to rise from the chair. Mike shoved him down cautioning him it was not wise.

The young girl put her face in her hands and began to sob uncontrollably. Her shoulders quivered as she hitched for air and tried to speak. "They... they..."

"Go ahead and take a few minutes. We won't let anything happen to you." Pam assured her and wrapped her arms around the young girl who buried her face in her chest. Pam gazed around the room tears filling her own eyes and she held the child close.

Mal was furious, writhing in his chair. Joe turned and marched for the room where the two men were tied up. Chris reached out and grabbed hold of him. "Listen Joe, don't go in there... you'll end up doing something you'll regret."

Joe turned and looked at him, rage filled his eyes, his nostrils flared, and he jerked his arm away from him. "They're the ones who are gonna regret what they've done."

I ran for the door to stop Joe, a man with a kind heart but ruled by his emotions. Arms out, as though these puny stems would stop the freight train coming my way, I closed my eyes and shouted. "Joe! Stop!" There was no hitch in his stride, he would not be stopped from giving these animals what they deserved. "JOE!" I screamed as loud as I could. The whole room paused and even Joe stopped and stared at me, eyes wide.

"You can't do this."

"I can, and I will. They're animals."

The little girl whimpered, and all eyes went to her. Joe's eyes softened and he turned to the little girl, his rage shifted to worry and concern. He moved toward her and knelt in front of her. His massive paws reaching out to hold the tiny hand. "Are you ready to tell us what happened?"

The little girl's eyes filled with tears that began to run down her reddened cheeks. She nodded her head and choked before she began to speak. "They came." Her voice hitched and she sucked in a ragged breath. "They came to our house. They asked my dad to come outside and help them with their truck. Me and my baby brother sat on the windowsill and watched while Daddy went out to help them. As soon as he got to the truck, two other men jumped out and hit him on the head. Then five men came in the house." Her sobs became incoherent, and she put her head in her hands.

Jen went over and held her. "Stop! The poor thing is terrified."

The little girl lifted her head and wiped her face. "My little brother... I need to help him."

Chris let out a breath he'd been holding with a loud gasp and stepped forward. "Susan. Is that your name?"

The child nodded and wiped her nose on her sleeve.

"Where do you live?"

"Gilsum."

"Do you know your address?"

Susan's head bobbed up and down. Pam hurried to her pack and fished around inside, grabbing a pen and pad; handing it to the girl who scratched the address on it. Holding it out to them, she waited.

"Let's go, Joe," Meeker walked past grabbing his arm.

"Wha?"

"You're coming with me to go to the little lady's house and check it out." He turned and glared at Chris. "Keep an eye on them." Pointing for the door to the small room where the two were tied up.

"I got this," Steve stepped up and headed for the door. "Doc, take a look at Mal. He ain't looking too healthy."

Joe grabbed his coat and gun and followed Meeker out the door.

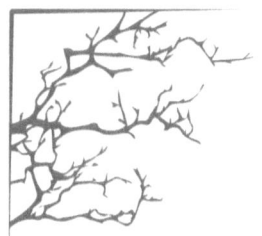

Sad Day

It was lunch time before the two came back, the young girl's mother and baby brother in tow. I looked past them hoping the girl's dad would follow in behind, but there was no one else. Susan ran to her mother, sobbing into her chest and hugging them. Her little brother looked to be about four and grabbed Susan's hand, gripping it as though he feared if he let go, she'd be gone.

Joe was still steaming mad, even more so than when he left. The woman, so thankful to be rescued, kept repeating, "Thank you."

Fawn led her over to the sofa. "Come and sit, why don't you rest here and then the kids can sit with you. Are you hungry?"

The woman followed her with some hesitation and sat in the far corner of the sofa curled up with her children, one under each arm. Her eyes hollow and full of fear, she scanned the room. I sat on the table in front of her and reached out, but she jerked her hand back in fear.

"You don't have anything to worry about. You're safe here. Can you tell us what happened?"

She buried her face in her children and began to cry, squeezing them so tight Sarah objected. "Mom, chill. They're nice."

I tousled the young boy's hair and stood. "When you're ready."

Pam called over from the kitchen, "Lunch is ready."

The woman looked up. We could see she was hungry. Susan squirmed from under her arm and tugged on her little brother. "C'mon Eddie, it's macaroni and cheese." Her hand seated in his, she raised her eyebrows at her mother, who released the child.

Her mother sat on the sofa subdued munching on a sandwich and chips. Seeming to relax some she ventured a few words. "My husband?"

Joe looked down and swung his head back and forth. "I'm sorry, ma'am."

The woman's eyes filled with tears, but they lingered on the bottom lash, suspended from falling by the last traces of mascara that had long ago been cried away. "I'd hoped, but deep down... I knew,"

I reached for her hand again. "We don't expect that you want to talk about everything, but can you tell us how many?"

She turned to me tilting her head. "How many?"

"Yes. Uh... Miss... How many attacked you? We want to be aware and be able to keep you and the kids safe."

She sat a bit straighter and brushed the crumbs from the front of her shirt. "I'm sorry, everything going on has been so overwhelming." The tears began to emerge again. "There were six of them, I think. The one that you killed back at the house," she looked to Joe. "He had three buddies that burst through the back door when my husband went outside. Then the two that took Susan." She paused, horror written across her face and stared at Susan. Her head snapped back to me, "Did they?"

"We don't believe so." I squeezed her hand and cast a glance at her daughter as she sat munching on her lunch and smiling playing with the other kids. "Just look at her, we didn't want to come right out and ask her, but she said they did not hurt her. I think they thought this house was abandoned but found out it was not."

Relief washed over the woman's body and her shoulders slumped. "I was terrified for her. The thought that..." Her voice cracked and trailed off, tears streaming down her face.

I turned to Chris and Joe, "I figure there is at least one more."

Mal shook his head, gazing upward counting in his head. "Two... There should be at least two more. I heard Susan talking earlier about a scary man when talking to the boys. She said he talked funny and ordered the rest around but remained outside when those two went in after killing her dad she saw him sitting in the truck when they took her away."

I paced, running the scenario through my head, trying to count when it dawned on me. "We need to stay alert because there could be more than that. I can't even figure out the count of who went into their house or not but one thing is clear, there is another that is somewhat in charge and this means there are more."

Steve, who'd been watching the men in the other room emerged, picking his fingernails with his knife, and looking like he'd just conquered Rome. "Well, our guests are awake and full of information."

We all stood waiting for Steve to share this information, but he seemed to be enjoying his spotlight and continued to pick at his nails as though there was nothing going on.

"Well?" Chris bellowed crossing the floor and waving a cup of coffee under his nose that he promptly pulled away when Steve reached for it.

"Well what?"

"Well what?" The room yelled out in unison. "What did they say?"

"Oh that." He sauntered across the floor to the sofa and looked right into Mal's eyes. "Do you know a guy named Mack Rogers?"

Mal's eyes widened, his face turned red, and he slammed his fists into the arm of the chair. "Don't you tell me he is involved."

Steve smirked and sneered. "And there's more."

Mal was fit to be tied, his face twisted into the angriest look I'd ever seen. "Spit it out," he cautioned Steve. "I am in no mood to guess."

"These guys? They're with the ones that burned down your house and blew up your truck."

I hopped up and stomped over to Steve. "The old woman?"

"From what they said, they were not personally involved with that, but they were at the house when the others did."

Now my blood was boiling. I stood up and marched for the room unholstering my gun. Mike tried to stop me, but I was ahead of him and burst through the door to the room where the two men were and I fired!

Jen gasped and Mal yelled, I heard them, but nothing registered except the memory of crawling away through the slushy red snow where the old woman had been killed. Mike reached me and took the gun from my hand as the tears welled up and stung my eyes. I sank to my knees sobbing. The memory of what these men had done would never leave me.

The man cried out in pain. "The bitch shot me!"

I glared at him and hissed, spit flying from my mouth. "A bullet is too good for either of you."

Mike hurried into the room where the men sat tied up and applied pressure to the wound. I'd shot him below the collar bone. Pam eyed the men and helped me from the floor, taking me over to where Mal was. I flopped down and cried into his knee. I was so furious that the tears flowed, no matter how hard I wanted to be.

The angry men cursed from the other room and taunted me. "You're gonna pay for this. Johan will make sure of that." A moment of silence fell on the room. "Ow, Doc, that hurt."

"It was supposed to. Just to let you know to take extreme care in who you threaten. While she was willing to just shoot you—I will save you, but only so that I can torture you later."

Mal winked at me, my breath hitching in my chest, I looked to the doorway. Mike emerged, wiping his hands, and winked at me. "I think they have seen the error in thinking they could threaten you Dani." He scanned the room and raised his chin to Meeker. "Or the rest of the women and children."

Meeker got up and went over to Mike who whispered something to him. He hurried to Chris and the two disappeared out the door.

"What did you...?" I started to ask but was silenced when Mike put his finger to his pursed lips. He sauntered over to Mal and I and whispered something in Mal's ear.

I was beginning to be upset when he leaned into my ear whispering, "We know where the others are." Steve and Joe went to the windows to scan the area and we waited for Meeker and Chris to return.

They'd gone to scout the information Mike had obtained with a bit of *chemical persuasion* as he'd called it. But we didn't want our newest guests to be frightened and kept it under wraps.

The kids played board games at the table while we shifted watches at the windows for a number of hours. Pam and Jen inventoried our supplies while Fawn paced, crying from time to time, worried about Meeker.

"Why does he always have to jump up and be the first one to go? I can't understand him, Dani."

I half laughed and half sighed... "If Mal wasn't all banged up it would be him out there alongside Meeker. We know how these guys are." I wrapped my arm around her shoulders. "Don't worry, Fawn, I know he will be careful. They are trying to protect us all. How about you and I start figuring out what to have for supper?"

She wiped the tears from her cheeks and offered a strained smile. Offering a squeeze of her hand I smiled back. "Besides, Meeker will be disappointed if there is nothing on the stove to snatch."

She snorted a laugh and snot oozed out of her nose. I gagged and scrunched my nose in disgust. "Eww, go grab a tissue." We began to giggle like schoolgirls and the others looked at us like we'd lost it, which made us giggle harder. The kids got in on the action and began to goof off, giggling and laughing, although they had no idea why.

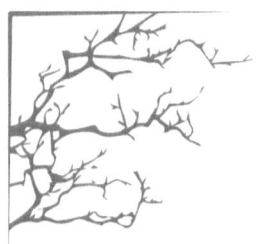

Time's Up

Mike and Steve continued to discover small bits of information from the two men. Some details were retrieved by means of chemical induction, while others were offered up out of sheer fear. Under normal circumstances I'd have been appalled by this, but now? I didn't care how we got the information we needed to survive.

Mack Rogers, it seemed, was part of an anarchist group that had been present at the violence and rioting all summer. They didn't care about issues; it was the chaos they were looking for. Their goal was to create chaos and they would start a fight for the highest bidder. There was no reasoning with this group and at times they seemed to be above the law. Johan was a code name for an unnamed government official... or group of them. I'm not sure these guys even knew; they wanted to cause havoc and do whatever they pleased and were only too happy to play their game. It was Mack that was behind much of the mayhem in our area. He and Mal had had run-ins before, which was why he was so mad when he heard his name.

Waiting for Meeker and Chris to return was getting harder by the minute, they'd been gone for hours. Fawn was no longer giggling but sat stoic in the corner, sure he was dead. Jen was also becoming worried about Chris and it showed on her face even though she tried to hide it from the boys.

I stared out the window at times and waited as the sun began to set and darkness crept across the white land. The moon offered enough light reflecting off the snow to see any movement in the trees. Even the trees seemed to be moving as I glared out the window from the dark cabin.

We didn't want any light showing through the windows to give away our position. The house was kept dark except for the kitchen, it had a single low lantern for light. The main room where everyone ate, the windows were boarded up and a dark blanket hung over its doorway. We all ate in shifts to keep watch and the kids still sat around the table in the kitchen munching their food. They'd been cooped up going on two days now and were getting antsy. Mal had moved back to the sofa and Mike and Steve were still in the room with the assailants. The small house was quiet and other than the smoke from the fire, no one would know it was occupied.

Keeping the fire hot reduced even the smoke, as the wood burned rather than smoldered, and with the blanket over the door it made the kitchen near sweltering. We were as stealthy as we could be, but our nerves were on edge. We expected Meeker and Chris to return before supper and both Fawn and Jen were beginning to panic.

I stood peering out the window thinking of the past three days when something caught my eye. I couldn't be sure, but I thought I saw something moving in the trees. I strained harder to see, but it was difficult to make out things in the dark. I saw it again... something moved from one tree to another. This could only be human; animals would not hide like this.

Joe motioned to me. "Did you see that?"

"I did."

"Keep an eye out, I'm going to get Steve." He stopped mid stride. "And Dani, be ready for anything."

"I will," my voice quivered.

I glared into the night, for the third time in two days we were being attacked. We had no idea if it was Meeker and Chris or the other's friends and the wait was agonizing. My muscles tensed and eyes strained to see anything in the darkness.

When the single knock echoed through the house Fawn screamed. She recovered herself when it was followed by the next two. Steve hurried to the door and unlatched it swinging it open.

Meeker stumbled in with Chris hanging from his arm. "Hurry, close the door and be ready."

Steve shut and locked the door, Pam and I settled the kids into the safe spot, propped Mal up in his chair with a clear line of sight to the door. The rest of us peered out the windows while Mike hurried to have a look at Chris.

He'd been shot in his upper thigh and had lost a bit of blood, but Meeker had used his belt as a tourniquet to stop the bleeding. Mike had Chris fixed up in no time. Everyone was on edge; the light was put out in the kitchen and we waited.

Those at the windows shifted every fifteen minutes because straining to see in the same spots too long and the trees themselves seemed to move. An hour passed and nothing appeared to be moving, we all began to relax.

Chris whispered waving in the scant moonlight. "Come here!"

I ran to the window and peered over the ledge. "I don't see anything."

"It could have been my eyes but look to the pine tree on the left while I go grab a sip of coffee."

"Gotcha."

Not even a minute passed when I too saw it. There was someone behind that tree. I grabbed my AR and peered through the scope watching the spot I'd seen the movement. Again, this time it was a face peering in our direction from behind the bull pine.

"Chris... Chris... Incoming!" I tipped my head to Joe at the other window to keep an eye on his side. Joe held his hand up pointing to the ceiling in the dim light and made a circle motion in the air. They were moving in. I saw them and still had a bead on the guy behind the tree.

In a flash from the muzzle, the barrage began. When that first shot rang out, I fired. The man slumped to the ground and I swung the rifle around to where a flash highlighted another. My hands shook and I had to breathe slowly to make the cross hairs quit dancing across the man's head. It centered, and I squeezed off another round. Swung it around to find another target.

"Dani, keep shooting."

"Be quiet Joe... You shoot your way; I'll shoot mine. I can't fire like you guys. I need to find the target and take a second to aim."

Meeker patted me on the back. "Do your thing, Dani, I've seen you shoot and only miss once in a thirty-round mag." He tipped his chin at Joe for a moment and went back to firing over my head.

A full thirty minutes we defended the barrage of gunfire that gradually subsided to the occasional pop. Meeker and Joe geared up to go check the situation and Fawn burst into tears. "Why must it always be you?"

"How else can I impress you?" He stroked her cheek and turned for the door.

"Hold up!" I peered through the scope breathed out and squeezed off one more round knocking a man from behind a too-small tree. Chris spotted him and fired. The man fell straight back.

"Alright you hacks make sure you know what you're shooting at."

"Wait..." I ran for my bag and grabbed a bottle of nail polish.

"What the hell you planning to do with that? Paint our nails?" Joe held his hand out as though he were admiring them.

Mal grinned at him. "Even you will be impressed with this one."

"Turn around," I demanded. I drew a dot about the size of a quarter on each ankle both sides of the foot. I had Jen hold a flashlight to each dot while it dried. Overall, it took about five minutes. "We will be able to identify that it is you out there, but it will only be visible when you lift your foot because of the snow." I sat back on my heels grinning at them.

"What the hell is it?" Meeker scrunched his nose.

"Nail polish. Glow in the dark."

"Told ya," Mal kicked back arms folded.

"Make sure if you stop for any length of time this dot is visible to the cabin, otherwise we will know to look at the feet of anyone walking. If you are visible and someone is creeping you, we can help out."

"Put a smaller dot on my ass." Meeker bent over.

"What? Why?"

"Cause if we need to be seen, best to have the dot more visible. I'd rather be shot in the ass than anywhere else."

Joe bent over beside him. I painted smaller dots about the size of a dime. I smacked them both on the ass when done. "Be careful out there."

"You guys pay attention where you're shooting."

There had been no gunfire during the entire time I was painting the guys with the nail polish. Neither Chris nor Steve had seen anything moving. We prayed all was clear but dared not hope as much. We all watched with held breath as the two dots made their way around the perimeter. Nothing else moved. After a thorough check of the area the two returned to the cabin. Everyone anxious about the news, waited for them to speak.

"Let's cover the windows and go ahead and light the lantern." Meeker looked at Fawn. "How about some of that coffee?"

She hurried off to get the pot from the wood stove while the two grabbed a seat on the sofa. Chris and I had the blankets up and lantern on in only a couple of minutes.

"First... anyone check on our two guests?"

Mike hopped up and headed for the room. It was freezing inside. His breath billowed into the air as a visible fog when he entered. He shined the flashlight inside onto the two men. They were riddled with bullet holes. We'd stacked firewood around the walls of the main room to hide behind but forgot to do so in the infirmary room.

"We noticed the bullet holes in the building on our sweep." Meeker sipped his steaming hot cup of coffee. "So, Dani... How many of them did you shoot?"

"I don't know. I aimed for the head; easier than shooting golf balls, but a lot more agonizing. I know one I got in the shoulder, but Chris finished him off. Why?"

"Well, we counted thirteen of them out there. Anyone left alive must have run off. But... nine of them were clean head shots and all on this side of the house. Two were around the back side, they left a blood trail with a couple holes in them. There is the one you both shot and another right in front of the window here." He pointed to the window I was positioned at with Joe." A bullet took off the top side of his head. Guess he peeked in at the wrong time.

My breath caught in my chest at the thought that they'd gotten so close, and my mind flashed back to that first intrusion with the break in where I'd shot the intruder. This time I felt nothing, not angry... not sad... nothing. These men had attacked us multiple times and killed the old woman. I was glad they were dead.

Joe plopped down on the sofa beside me, flinging his arm over my shoulder. "You can be on my team anytime."

I flung it off. "Knock it off."

"What about the vehicles?" Mal was not ready to celebrate our win quite yet.

"They're fine. But... there is also an abandoned Humvee on the path with the keys dangling in the ignition."

"Great..." I stood up. "That makes up for Mal's truck."

The men bickered back and forth about what to do. Our location had been compromised and we'd decided it was time to leave, but the question was to where? We'd thought this location was safe, but it fast became evident that it was not.

Chris and Mike thought we should go into the Andora forest and hide out. Mal and Joe thought we should head north, while it was my opinion that we needed to head south. It was only a few weeks into winter and New England could be brutally cold. Several of our houses had been burned and with Meeker's trailer taken over, we had no place to go to shelter from the weather. All of Keene was gone and it was not likely the Veterinary clinic survived. Steve and Pam's house was intact last anyone checked but it was not likely it would remain safe.

We had no plan for this...

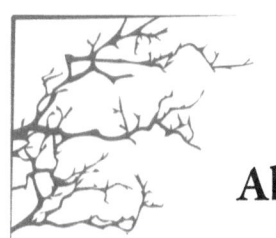

About the Author

D J Cooper is the author of the Dystopia series, Insurrection Series, Nine Meals from Anarchy, and other short works. Currently a student at Southern New Hampshire University.

Often writing humor, or research articles for POSH Prepper's Podcast and others, she keeps up on things for her post-apocalyptic fiction. She can be found in front of a computer somewhere, favoring the outdoors when writing.

Works by the Author

Dystopia Series
Beginning of the End
The Long Road
Revelations
The Dark Days
Insurrection Series
Deception
Abolition
Evasion
Nine Meals from Anarchy
Sun's Fury
Terminus State
Next Nine Meals Book (July 2021)

Contact the Author

Email:
DJCooper.Author@gmail.com

Web:
Https://authoroftheapocalypse.com

Social Media:

Twitter   Djcooper2015

Skype   DJcooper2015

Facebook   AuthorDJCooper

TikTok   @authordjcooper

Instagram   djcooper_authorofapoc

www.ingramcontent.com/pod-product-compliance
Lightning Source LLC
Chambersburg PA
CBHW020141180626
46810CB00004B/1663